D1098315

3

HOME IS WHERE THE HEART IS

Jayne and Dan Pearson have moved to their dream house . . . a huge dilapidated heap on top of a Cornish cliff. The stresses of city life are behind them, their children consider their new home 'the coolest house ever', and the family's future looks rosy. But when a serious accident forces them to re-think their dream, they embark upon a completely different way of life — though its pleasures and disasters bring a whole new meaning to the word *stress* . . .

CHRISSIE LOVEDAY

HOME IS WHERE THE HEART IS

Complete and Unabridged

LINFORD
Leicester

First published in Great Britain in 2007

First Linford Edition
published 2007

British Library CIP Data

Loveday, Chrissie
    Home is where the heart is.—Large print ed.—
Linford romance library
    1. Cornwall (England: County)—Fiction
    2. Love stories
    3. Large type books
    I. Title
    823.9′2 [F]

    ISBN 978–1–84782–035–8

Published by
F. A. Thorpe (Publishing)
Anstey, Leicestershire

Set by Words & Graphics Ltd.
Anstey, Leicestershire
Printed and bound in Great Britain by
T. J. International Ltd., Padstow, Cornwall

This book is printed on acid-free paper

Catastrophe

'That was the coolest party ever, and this is the coolest house!' Carl shouted in excitement.

'You certainly all seemed to enjoy yourselves,' said Jayne Pearson, Carl's mum, feeling utterly exhausted.

The 'coolest party ever' seemed to have been going on for ever, and she desperately needed a sit down, and several cups of tea, before she could even begin to feel human again.

When Carl and his sister, Sarah, had asked if they could have a sleepover party for their friends, it had seemed like a reasonable idea. The house, which the Pearsons had only moved into recently, was still in a mess, with only the minimum number of rooms habitable, and Carl, at the boisterous age of thirteen, had assured his parents that his mates would love staying over. They could have 'awesome' games with very little furniture around. Sarah, who was twelve, had been equally enthusiastic, and so the party had been arranged.

The bumps and giggles had lasted most of the night, and Jayne and Dan had been kept awake late into the night, listening to it all.

Now, breakfast over, the last of the seemingly endless mob of boys and girls had left, after eating mountains of cornflakes, drinking gallons of milk, and consuming enough slices of toast to keep a small army going.

'OK, you two, grab a bin-bag each and let's get cleared up,' commanded Jayne. 'What a mess,' she said, with a sigh. 'Mind you, I should be used to living in a shambles, by now.'

A few months ago, buying this house, Sea Haven, had felt like a dream come true.

Sea Haven had been on the market for a long, long time, because of it being both in a state of disrepair and too large for most people, but the structure of the old house was sound, and Dan and and Jayne had felt confident that they could turn it into their dream home.

Overlooking a pretty bay in their beloved Cornwall, the ramshackle house was going to become the family home that the Pearsons had always longed for.

Sea Haven had originally been a small hotel which had then become an old folks' home until the regulatory bodies had closed it down for not coming up to the required standards.

The building had remained empty and unloved for some years, and Dan and Jayne Pearson's family and friends had thought they'd taken leave of their senses when they'd left their comfy modern bungalow for this decaying heap.

But buying Sea Haven was to be the start of a new life for the family, away from the stresses and strains of the city.

Dan certainly wouldn't miss working in the city, scrabbling for the last parking place each morning after a long drive through traffic.

'I'll be able to work from home,' he'd told his colleagues. 'Accountants can work from anywhere, these days. And Jayne can be my secretary again, just as she was when we first met.'

It would be risky having to build up a new client base, but Dan felt confident that he would be able to make a good living for them all. And although there was a lot of money needed to be spent on Sea Haven, they planned to do most of the work themselves to keep the costs down.

'Once we get it straight, we could even take in guests for bed and breakfast,' Jayne had suggested. 'As the surveyor told us, most of the work we need to do is cosmetic. The decorations are hideous, but a few rolls of wallpaper and some paint will soon sort that.'

'Yes, well, taking in guests for bed and breakfast can be Plan B, if the accountancy business is less than successful,' Dan had agreed.

The children loved the house and

were in seventh heaven.

Their school in Truro was still within reach of their new home if they travelled by car, so they were able to keep the same friends, and there was space enough for their friends to visit and stay over.

'Did you see what James did when . . .'

'Shut up, Sarah,' Carl hissed. 'We don't want you-know-who to hear.'

'We haven't been struck deaf, you know,' Jayne said, hiding a smile. 'Though with all that so-called music blaring out, I don't know how. I'm surprised we didn't get the neighbours round complaining.'

'But we don't have neighbours,' Sarah said with a grin. 'That's why this place is so cool.'

'All the better for nobody to hear your screams when we tickle you,' laughed Dan. 'Come here, you.'

He chased the yelling pair around until everyone collapsed in a hysterical heap.

'All right, you lot,' said Jayne. 'Half an hour till lunch and I want every scrap of rubbish, every paper plate and drinks can collected up and put in the correct recycling boxes. OK. Move it.' Jayne could look very fierce when she wanted to.

'Yes, M'am. Certainly, M'am.' Dan saluted. 'Come on, troops. Get to it. Bin-bags at the ready.'

As Jayne began preparing lunch, Dan came up behind her and put his arms around her waist.

'The kids really had a great time, didn't they?' he said. 'We did do the right thing, moving here, didn't we?'

'Yes, we did,' she replied firmly. 'Good job we had the inheritance though, or we'd have been very short of cash for the renovations.'

'Good old Uncle Joseph. Who'd have thought he'd remember you from all those years ago?'

Jayne's inheritance had come right out of the blue, a few months back, when Uncle Joseph had left Jayne a substantial amount of money. She'd felt slightly guilty at the time, as she couldn't really remember the old man who was not even a proper uncle. He'd been some sort of distant cousin of her grandparents, and although she'd sometimes visited him when she was a child, she'd seen nothing of him since she'd grown up.

He'd had a collection of rare stamps, which had been sold for a considerable amount of money, and Jayne had been the only surviving relative from that side of the family.

It had been Jayne's inheritance that had clinched the Pearsons' plans to buy Sea Haven.

'I'm going to clean out the guttering after lunch,' Dan announced. 'There's rain forecast and it leaked all down the side of the house last time there was a storm.'

'Shouldn't we get someone in to do it? It's quite a height.'

'Don't fuss. It's no problem. You can stand at the bottom and hold the ladder steady.'

'Well, if you're sure it's safe. Just

promise not to land on top of me if you do fall.'

⋆　⋆　⋆

Over lunch, Dan remembered something. 'I meant to tell you. When Mum rang, she said Chloe's back in the country.'

'Where's Auntie Chloe been for so long?' Carl asked. 'We haven't seen her for years.'

'She's been in Malaysia, working with orphaned children.'

Dan's younger sister had given up her university course after a couple of years, and taken herself off on voluntary service overseas. The family had been somewhat surprised at her decision, but she'd been enthusiastic about the project and had been away for almost four years.

'She'll have a huge culture shock when she tries to settle again,' Jayne commented. 'What does she plan to do?'

'You know Chloe. Nobody could ever tell her what to do. But she must be twenty-six now, and well able to look after herself.'

Dan had been sixteen when his sister was born and, at the time, he'd had a lot of mixed feelings about this unexpected addition to the family.

First, there'd been the shock of discovering that his parents were still capable of having a baby and then, the unexpected emotion of seeing the tiny baby smile at him.

He'd been won over instantly, though he'd had to keep his delight hidden from his friends who would have teased him unmercifully if they'd known the pleasure he got from giving Chloe her bottle.

'Maybe Chloe could come and stay with us, once we're straight,' Jayne suggested.

'That'll take years. We'll never see her if we wait that long,' Dan said, laughing. 'Anyway, I have to get on now. I'll set up the ladder and give you a call when I'm ready.'

'If you must, but, Dan, seriously, can't we get someone to come in? I'm worried. You're not used to ladders and . . . '

'Stop worrying. I'll be fine. Come on, kids. You can help.'

'Do we have to?' they moaned.

'Come on. We spent all last night listening to you enjoying yourselves. The least you can do is help us now.'

'But I've got homework to do,' Carl announced.

'Then you can do it tomorrow. Since when did you ever do homework on a Saturday? You always leave it until as late as possible on Sunday. But I'll bear it in mind. Perhaps you're turning over a new leaf and getting it done before the last minute.'

'OK. What do we have to do?'

'Get buckets, a trowel and some rope. I'll haul a bucket up after me, fill it with the gunge from the guttering, then I lower it down to you two. You can have the pleasure of emptying it and sending it back up to me.'

'Aw, gross,' Sarah said, with a horrified expression.

* * *

Jayne loaded the dishwasher and took some meat out of the freezer to thaw for the evening meal. No sooner was one meal over than you had to plan for the next, she thought, as she wiped down the kitchen worktop.

She could hear the family outside, laughing and shouting to each other, and she smiled as she pulled on a jacket. The wind was blowing off the sea and still had bite to it, despite the early spring sunshine.

'So, how's it going?' she asked as she came round the corner. 'Hey, what are you doing up there, Dan? I thought I was supposed to be steadying the ladder?'

'It's OK, you don't need to. It's quite safe on this side of the house. I can grab the drainpipe if I think I'm going to fall.'

She watched as he scooped out the gritty black mud and filled the bucket. Carefully, he lowered it to the waiting children who then tied on a second bucket. Pulling faces, they went off to empty the first.

'Looks as if you're organised and don't need me. I'll go and tidy that flower bed at the side. Be careful, though — all of you.'

Jayne pottered off to the border where a few daffodils were struggling through, their spiky buds heralding better weather to come. She pictured a mass of lovely flowers, stretching right down the drive as far as the gate. But for now, there were just a few survivors from earlier days. The huge garden had been neglected for several years, but one day, she decided, as well as a profusion of flowers, there would be beds for all kinds of vegetables. She would grow all that they needed for themselves, but a lot of work lay ahead.

Jayne set to it. She began by tugging out a few weeds by hand but she really needed her garden fork and her hoe, and set off to fetch them.

Round the other side of the house, the guttering was evidently finished and Dan was climbing down the long ladder.

'See?' he said, grinning. 'That was no problem. I'll make a DIY expert yet. I'll move along and do the next bit.'

He tried to move the ladder but it had somehow jammed against the drainpipe. 'Drat. I'll have to go back up and try to release it. It's slipped behind the pipe.'

'But how can you move it if you're standing on it?' protested Jayne, as he climbed back up to the dizzying height. Her heart was thumping as she watched, and a dark foreboding raced through her mind.

She watched fearfully as Dan bounced the ladder, trying to release it. He shouldn't do that, it was dangerous . . . He shouldn't . . . Her worst fears were realised. The ladder swayed and Dan came crashing to the ground.

Everything seemed to go into slow motion as Sarah screamed and Carl dropped the bucket and came racing back to the house. Dan wasn't moving and his legs were folded under him at an unnatural angle. Jayne bent over him, calling his name and trying to feel for a pulse.

'Shouldn't we try to straighten his legs?' Sarah sobbed. 'He looks so uncomfortable.'

'No, Sarah. He mustn't be moved at all,' said Carl. 'Shall I call an ambulance, Mum?'

'Please, love. And make sure they know exactly where we are. Tell them to hurry.'

Carl rushed away, and Jayne pulled off her jacket, laying it gently over her unconscious husband. Tears were threatening, but she had to be strong for the children's sake, and it certainly wouldn't help anyone if she panicked.

'Is he breathing?' stammered Sarah.

'Of course he is,' Jayne said fiercely, praying she was right.

It seemed ages before Carl came out of the house again.

'They're on their way. Should be about ten minutes. I said I'd go down the hill to show them the way. How is he?' he asked, shakily.

'He's unconscious. Don't worry, Carl, the paramedics will know what to do when they get here.'

'But he will be all right, won't he?' Carl asked.

'Oh yes, I'm sure he will be, love.'

He has to be all right — he has to be! Jayne thought, desperately.

★   ★   ★

An absolute age passed before they heard a siren approaching along the beach road. Carl came running back up the drive with the ambulance, which drew up as near to them as it could.

The paramedics quickly assessed the problem and began to treat Dan, who was still unconscious. They took the utmost care as they strapped on a neck support and fitted an oxygen mask over his face.

Jayne thought she was about to pass out herself. She was hanging on to her tears, not wanting the children to see her break down.

'We'll soon have him at the hospital and they'll do a proper assessment there,' one of the paramedics was saying, reassuringly.

'Can I come with him?' Jayne asked, and then realised she could hardly leave Carl and Sarah.

'Better if you follow us. It'll be some time before they can begin any treatment, so don't hurry. Get yourself sorted out here, and then come to the hospital. You'd best get someone to look after the children for now. Hospitals can be disturbing places for youngsters, especially the emergency room.'

'Yes, yes, of course,' Jayne muttered, not hearing anything properly as thoughts raced round her mind. What if . . . What if?

They stood in a tight little knot,

watching as they packed Dan into the ambulance and drove him away.

'Oh, Mum,' Carl said, grabbing on to her arm. 'What are we going to do?'

'We're going to phone one of your school friends and ask if you can go and stay while I go to the hospital. Who do you suggest?'

'But we want to go with you,' protested Sarah. 'We want to know what's happening.'

'I know, love, but you heard what the ambulance man said. If I know you're being looked after, I'll be able to concentrate on what I'm doing. And I can keep phoning you. Now, who shall I ask?'

'S'pose Luke and Emily's mum would be best,' said Carl. 'Sarah and Emily are mates as well as me and Luke.' He looked across at his sister, who nodded, unhappily, in agreement. Only a few hours ago, they'd all said goodbye after a great party.

Jayne went to call Claire — Luke and Emily's mum — who was a good friend

17

of the whole family, and arranged to drop the children off on her way to the hospital.

'Get your pyjamas and toothbrushes. And take your homework with you. You may be there tomorrow as well. Keep your mobiles switched on.'

They all rushed around the house, grabbing essentials, and only ten minutes after the ambulance had left they were piling into the car, ready to go.

Jayne took several deep breaths and made a supreme effort to steady her shattered nerves. An overwhelming feeling of panic was threading through her entire body. What if he didn't regain consciousness?

What if . . . ? What if . . . ? What if . . . ? Control yourself, she ordered.

'OK? All strapped in? Got everything you need?'

'Haven't got school clothes,' Sarah said, in a little voice, hardly more than a whisper.

'Don't worry. If we're not back home

tomorrow, I'll bring them round to Claire's.'

★ ★ ★

When she arrived at the hospital, Jayne was told that Dan had regained consciousness. He was in a great deal of pain, both his legs were broken, and it was a possibility that there had been some spinal damage as well.

It was such relief to Jayne to know that Dan was conscious that she barely took in the implications of the rest.

'Can I see him?' she begged.

'Of course. I'll take you through,' the doctor said. 'But he's fairly drowsy after the pain relief. Don't expect too much.'

'Hello, love,' Dan whispered. 'You were right. We should have got someone in to clean out the guttering.'

'Oh, Dan. Thank heavens you're conscious. I was dreading . . . well, I was imagining all sorts, on the drive over.'

'They won't let me come home,' he

complained, in a small, quiet voice. 'They want to keep me in for a few days.'

'I know. Try not to talk too much. The kids send their love . . . '

Dan's face was positively grey and he seemed to be slipping into a deep sleep.

'We need to get him to the scanner now, to make certain there's no brain damage,' the doctor told her gently. 'Don't worry — it's a routine precaution in the case of a fall like this. But I suspect we shall be keeping him in for some time, not just for a few days. We think he's probably fractured his pelvis and, as I said, there could be spinal damage, too. But, it's much too early to say definitely. We'll get the scan organised and then some X-rays. Why don't you go and get a cup of tea? I'll ask the nurse to show you to the relatives' room.'

Jayne nodded. She felt numb as she followed the nurse along the corridor to the relatives' room, where she was left to sit alone with a cup of tea.

By the time she'd counted the floor tiles twice, and the wall tiles at least three times, she thought she'd go mad, and went outside to call the children. She told Carl and Sarah, truthfully, that their father was conscious but that he'd broken both his legs and would have to stay in hospital for a while.

'When can we see him?' Sarah asked.

'Tomorrow, perhaps. Once he's on the ward. You'll be able to sign his plastered legs and draw all over them.' She managed to raise a weak laugh from her daughter. 'Now, can you put Claire on, please?'

Jayne came off the phone feeling reassured that her friend didn't mind looking after the children — that was one less thing to worry about during that long, lonely evening. All she could think of was Dan, and how they were going to cope.

At best it was going to be a long recuperation. At worst, he could be wheel-chair bound . . . for weeks . . . months

— or even for ever. Her hands shook so much that she spilled her lukewarm tea.

Who'd have thought, this morning, that all this was waiting round the corner?

Facing The Past

It seemed an endless wait for news. Occasionally, a nurse looked into the relatives' room to see how Jayne was doing, smiled, and went away again. Eventually, a doctor arrived.

'Mrs Pearson, you'll be relieved to hear that there seems to be no brain damage at all. But your husband does have a crack in his pelvis, as well as two broken legs. Fortunately, there is no sign of any damage to his spine, so he should make a full recovery, but it is going to take a very long time. You'll need to prepare yourself for him having a long stay in hospital and he might need to spend some time in a rehabilitation unit.'

'But you do think he should be able to walk again?' Jayne asked in a trembling voice.

'In time, yes, we hope so. But there

are never any guarantees with this type of injury. He's been taken to the ward, if you'd like to see him?'

She followed the doctor, asking herself endless questions as she thought of the implications of what she'd been told.

How would she cope with everything that needed to be done to their new home? What would they live on if Dan wasn't able to earn any money? Her mind was whirling.

'Hello, love. Hope it isn't too painful,' she whispered, as she sat down at Dan's bedside.

He looked ghastly, lying white faced against the hospital pillows. A large cage structure was covering his legs and he wore a hospital gown. Various drips were attached to his arms.

'Jayne, I've made a mess of everything. I'm sorry. I should have listened to you — got someone in.' His voice was almost a whisper.

'It could have been worse. You could have been killed.' Jayne swallowed hard.

'Oh, my love, I'm so sorry it had to happen. But you'd better get some rest now. I'll go and see the kids and I'll be back tomorrow. Have a good rest now.' She kissed him and, blinking away her tears, left him to sleep.

'What's next?' she asked the doctor, on her way out of the ward.

'We'll see how he is tomorrow, and then he'll have his legs put in plaster. They're in temporary splints at the moment while we work out exactly how best to treat him. You can visit any time after twelve tomorrow. By then, we'll have decided what to do. Now, I suggest you get yourself home and try to rest.'

★　★　★

As she drove home, Jayne's mind was racing. How were they going to earn any money? She thought about her suggestion to Dan, that she could take in bed and breakfast guests during the holiday season. But for her to be able to do that, the house would have to be in decent order, and they'd hardly made a start on it yet.

It was now the beginning of March, so in a few weeks the first visitors would be arriving in Cornwall. If Dan was unable to work for some months, it seemed sensible to get moving with the work on the house.

Before she went home, Jayne called in at Claire's to see the children. They were ready for bed, so Jayne decided they should stay over, as planned. Once they were in bed, she and Claire sat talking for a while.

'You can stay, as well, if it helps,' her friend offered. 'It would have to be the couch, but you might prefer it to an empty house.'

Jayne shook her head. 'I'd better get back. I gave the hospital our home phone number, but I need to get back anyway. I'm not sure I locked up properly.'

'If you're sure you'll be OK? It's a big empty place.'

But Jayne knew that she needed to be at home. She would collect the children next morning, and they could go with her to visit Dan. Longer term plans could wait. She thanked Claire, and drove the five miles back to Sea Haven.

★　★　★

It seemed strange to be alone in the big bed. She and Dan had rarely spent a night apart, and she felt a cold draught down his side of the bed.

She put his pillow alongside her, and hugged it for comfort.

Jayne lay awake, fretting, and finally dozed off in the small hours of the morning, dreaming strange dreams that merged with the reality of the day that had gone.

She awoke at eight o'clock the next morning, amazed to find that she had actually slept for so long. Immediately, she reached for the phone and called the hospital.

'Your husband passed a comfortable

night, and he's fine this morning,' the ward nurse told her.

How could Dan have been comfortable? How could he be fine?

'So, when can I bring the children in to see him?'

'Oh, well, we don't encourage children on the ward.'

'They're not little children. Carl's thirteen and Sarah's twelve and if it's going to be a long-term recovery, they need to see their father or they'll think there's more going on than we're telling them.'

Jayne felt tears threatening as she argued, struggling to keep control.

'It's all right, Mrs Pearson. Of course you can bring the children in to see their father. It's just that it could be distressing for them to be in a hospital at all, let alone visiting someone with various bits of equipment attached. You'd best leave visiting until later in the day, though. The consultant will be round any time now and they might decide to operate right away. We'll give you a call later.'

Jayne put the phone down and stared at it, tears rolling down her cheeks. If only she'd insisted on getting someone in to clear the wretched gutters. If only . . . If only . . .

'Stop this,' she told herself firmly. 'Pull yourself together and start to act rationally.'

She showered and went downstairs.

It was only then that she realised how hungry she was. She scrambled some eggs and made toast.

Then she made a casserole from the meat that she'd taken out of the freezer yesterday, and put it into the Aga to cook slowly. The kids would need a meal when they got home.

The phone began to ring.

'Mum? How's Dad?'

'Hello, Carl. He's doing OK. I called the hospital and we might be able to visit this afternoon.'

'He is going to be all right, isn't he?'

'They think so, but it'll take a long time.'

'All right. Sarah wants to speak to you now.'

Jayne reassured her daughter and then asked to speak to Claire.

'Thanks so much for helping out,' she said softly.

'It's no problem, Jayne. Now, listen, I've organised Sunday lunch for everyone so please come round as soon as you're ready.'

Jayne began to protest, but Claire cut her short.

'Just get yourself over here and stop arguing.'

Before setting off for Claire's, Jayne did some tidying and put out the rubbish that still remained after the party.

Her head began to clear a little as she wandered round the house, going from room to room and studying the general condition of the place. She made mental notes of the various decorating jobs that needed to be done, and the furniture she might need, to get a bed and breakfast business up and running.

Then she packed up a few of Dan's things to take to the hospital.

Feeling much more positive, she set off for lunch at Claire's.

★ ★ ★

Sarah was visibly shocked at the sight of her father lying in a hospital bed, his legs encased in plaster casts and attached to a series of pulleys.

'Hi kids. Looks like I won't be playing football for a while.' He smiled feebly and held out his hand to them all. 'Hey, it's OK. I can just about manage a hug so long as you do the bending.'

'Oh, Dad . . . ' said Sarah, the tears filling her eyes.

'Can I sign your plaster?' Carl asked, trying to be cheerful.

'Nothing rude, thank you.' Dan smiled. 'So, how's everything at home?'

'Fine. We stayed at Luke and Emily's last night. And Mum came over to their house for lunch today.'

Jayne leaned over and gave him a hug. 'Missed you last night,' she whispered.

'They gave me something to make me sleep, so I don't remember much,' said Dan. He tapped his plaster cast and grimaced. 'This could stop me from clearing gutters out for some time.'

'For ever, if I have my way,' Jayne retorted with feeling.

They all chatted more easily as the visit went on, but Dan was soon worn out. He kept closing his eyes and Jayne was unsure whether it was the medication, or if he was just too tired to speak.

'I think we should leave you to rest now,' she said, the third time he seemed to be drifting off.

'Sorry. I don't seem to be able to keep my eyes open,' he said, gripping her hand as if he was afraid to let it go.

'I'll be back to visit you tomorrow. But I think it may be best if I come before I pick up the kids from school. They'll have homework and mustn't be too late to bed.'

'We want to see Dad, too,' protested Carl. 'And they'll give us special treatment at school, under the circumstances — you know, let us off homework and stuff.'

'They'll do no such thing! We'll organise a couple of visits during the week, but I want things to go on as normally as possible.' Jayne was adamant.

'Don't worry about anything, love,' she whispered to Dan. 'We'll keep things going, and you'll be home before you know it.'

'It'll maybe take a bit longer than that. I'm sorry, love, I've been very stupid.'

'Hush,' she said, putting her finger to his lips. 'I'll see you tomorrow.'

The children gave their father big hugs and tiptoed out of the ward, somehow feeling the need to creep out quietly, despite the racket of trolleys and the chatter that was going on all around them.

'Oh, Mum, everything's a mess, isn't it?' Sarah whispered, her voice thick with threatening tears. Her eyes, exactly the same colour of hazel as Dan's, were red-rimmed.

'At least we know Dad's going to be all right, even if life's not quite going according to plan. We shall have to think how we're going to deal with all this. We'll talk about it over supper. Oh, heavens!'

'What? What's the matter?'

'I put supper in the Aga this morning and forgot to take it out when Claire invited us for lunch.'

'I couldn't eat much anyway,' Carl assured her. 'After Claire's lunch, all I want is some toast or something.'

'That's fine by me. All the same, we shouldn't waste food. Money's going to be a bit short from now on.'

No-one said much as they drove home, all deep in thought.

Whatever happened, Jayne was determined that she wouldn't allow the children to worry any more than they had to. She must keep cheerful. If she had to feel down at any time, it could only happen at night when the children were safely in bed.

'Does Granny know what's happened?' Carl asked, as they stopped outside the house.

Jayne gasped. She'd been so wound up in what was happening, she hadn't even thought of contacting Dan's mother! Her scatty mother-in-law wouldn't be of much help, but she had to be told.

'Not yet, I thought I'd phone her tonight. I didn't want to worry her until we knew Dad would be all right.'

The small fib made it sound as if she was being thoughtful. In truth, she rather dreaded breaking the news to Flora.

'I could phone Granny if you like,' Sarah offered.

'Well, that's very nice of you, dear, but I ought to do it really.'

'But you know what Granny's like,' said Sarah, 'She'll go into overdrive trying to cope with it. I'll call her. She'll be better with me. You know she will.'

'You're growing up, Sarah,' Jayne muttered, surprised by her daughter's insight. 'Thank you, darling. You're quite right. I'll go and scrape out the supper while you ring her.'

An Unexpected Arrival

As predicted, Dan's mother took the news badly. What could she do to help? Would Dan really be able to walk again? Were they going to sell the house? Would Jayne have to go out to work? What were they hiding from her?

Helplessly, Sarah held out the phone to her mother. '*Sorry*,' she mouthed.

'Flora, how are you?' Jayne asked.

'Rather under the weather, if I'm truthful. The damp plays havoc with my arthritis. But I'm managing. Now, how is Daniel, really?'

'He's getting on quite well, but he'll be in hospital for some weeks.'

'How on earth will you manage? Is that awful place you've bought actually habitable?'

'Of course it is. It needs a lot doing to it but it's basically sound and most things seem to work. The children think it's absolutely wonderful and so do Dan and I.'

'Hmm,' Flora murmured, obviously preferring to believe that Sea Haven was a rat-infested, dry-rot-riddled slum — a quite unsuitable place for her grandchildren to be brought up.

'Well, Jayne, I really feel that I ought to offer to come and help you. Cook meals for you and such like.'

'I wouldn't dream of asking you,' Jayne said quickly.

The idea of Flora bumbling round her kitchen, and complaining about the mess the house was in, didn't bear thinking about.

'It's really good of you to offer, but at the moment we're coping very well. Besides, if your arthritis is playing up . . . ' she floundered. 'In any case, the children are at school all day and there's lots for me to do here. Perhaps when Dan's home again?'

'Well, if you're sure.'

Jayne smiled to hear the relief in her mother-in-law's voice.

'Once we've got a nice room ready for you, it will be lovely to see you. I'm planning to get on with the decorating as soon as possible.'

'I hope you aren't making a huge mistake. I was always a bit doubtful about you taking on such a place. Wouldn't it be sensible to sell it and buy a nice little bungalow somewhere with the proceeds?'

'We'd be lucky to buy anything at all for what we'd get for this place. Taking all the costs of moving into consideration, we'd make a huge loss if we tried to sell it again. Besides, with all these bedrooms, we'll be able to take in guests if necessary. Look, I must go and get supper for the children. I'll call again as soon as there's any news about Dan.'

Jayne put down the phone before Flora could say any more.

'Sorry, Mum, I couldn't quite manage to deal with her. She just goes on and on, doesn't she?' Sarah apologised.

'Come and give me a hug, you

gorgeous girl,' Jayne said, pulling her daughter close. Carl came and joined them and the three of them stood in the silent kitchen, united in their worries about the immediate future.

'What this place needs is some cheerful music,' Carl announced.

'Oh no,' Jayne cried. 'Not your awful music.' But it was too late — a thumping beat rang out from his CD player.

'It does cheer the place up, you must admit.' He laughed.

'You're right. Now, let's see the state of the delicious casserole I made so lovingly.'

★　★　★

Two days of soaking with every chemical product known to man removed most of the burnt mess from the pan. And in those two days, they all seemed to come to terms with the changes in the household.

Dan was also coming to terms with

things, though it didn't stop him from worrying about how they would manage. Jayne told him repeatedly that everything was going to be all right, but he wasn't happy that decisions were being made without him.

'If only the timing had been different,' he moaned. 'Up to six weeks ago, I had an insurance policy that would have covered us for all of this.'

'But we both of us took the decision to discontinue it. We both decided that it was an unnecessary expense in the circumstances. Anyway, they'd probably have found some reason not to pay out. Let's face it, climbing high ladders doesn't fit into an accountant's normal job description.' Jayne tried to reason with him. 'We're OK for money for a while. And I'm going to start on the decorating and see what needs doing regarding the plumbing — en-suite bathrooms and such. In a few weeks' time, I could be taking in B and B guests. That has to help with the finances, doesn't it?'

'Well, it'll make a dent, but you'll exhaust yourself. Then where will we all be? We've got the money your Uncle Joseph left you to use on the house. You don't need to rush into taking in guests.'

'For goodness' sake, Dan, just stop worrying and raising objections to everything. Now, I'd better go and collect the children. I'll bring them in to see you tomorrow, so expect us a bit later. Is there anything you need?'

'Leave me a few coins, will you? I'll buy a paper in the morning when the trolley comes round.'

She kissed him and squeezed his hand tightly. 'Love you,' she whispered. She felt a lump in her throat and knew that it was time to leave. Dan must never see her cry or even looking sad — she needed to be strong for all of them.

The hospital corridor was already becoming familiar to her, and she spoke to a couple of other visitors as they passed. It was frightening how quickly one became used to the routine, she thought.

While the children did their homework that evening, Jayne sat with a notepad and several sticky labels. She took a separate sheet of paper for each room, and began to list everything that needed to be done. On the sticky labels she wrote what she would need to buy and attached them to each page in turn.

'Undercoat, emulsion, gloss — how do you work out how many rolls of wallpaper you need for a room?'

She muttered to herself about pasting tables and paper hanging brushes. Did they have any? If so, where were they? Or would she need to buy them?

'Mum, are you going to mutter on all night or can we have hush while we're doing our homework? Or maybe we can have some music on to drown you out?'

'Sorry.'

'What are you doing anyway?' Sarah asked.

'Making lists of what needs to be done in every room and then trying to work out how much the materials will cost.'

'Wow — does that mean you're going to do it all yourself?'

'I'll need some help. Some of the plumbing will need replacing and repairing. And we're going to put in en-suite bathrooms for each of the rooms. I certainly couldn't do that.'

'We could have a peeling party at the weekend,' Sarah said. 'You know — invite a few people round to help peel off the old wallpaper. It could be fun.'

'And who, might I ask, is going to want to come and peel off old wallpaper?'

'Leave it to us,' Sarah said, her eyes shining with inspiration. 'All you have to do is buy a load of pizzas and we'll organise the rest.'

'I'm not sure, Sarah. Let me think

about it. It's a bit soon to be stripping off all the wallpaper.'

'Is this the same woman who only minutes ago was making endless lists and mumbling about pots of paint?'

Carl sounded so like his father that Jayne burst out laughing.

'Give me tomorrow to get my mind sorted, and we'll see.'

The two children slapped their hands together crying out, '*Yes!*'

'I only said that we'll see,' Jayne said anxiously. 'Don't get carried away!'

'It's the only possible solution, Mum. We get all the walls stripped off and you do the painting or papering . . . job done. You always say that getting ready to do a job is the worst part. And the supermarket does happen to have a special on pizzas — I saw the advert last night.'

Jayne thought about their idea as she lay in the bath that evening, soaking away the day's worries.

It might just work. In any case, it would please the children and make them feel more involved.

She had to plan properly for the things the house needed, like hand basins and the en-suite bathrooms for some of the rooms . . . extra furniture, sheets and towels . . . and whether the old washing machine would cope with so much washing.

Whatever happened, even if they didn't become a bed and breakfast establishment, the house was going to have to be decorated.

Jayne decided that she'd tell the kids at breakfast that they could go ahead with their plans for a 'peeling party'.

Jayne topped-up the bath with hot water, lay back, and sighed. Somewhere in the middle of all this frantic activity, she would have to fit in visits to the hospital to see Dan.

Life was certainly proving hectic at the moment!

* * *

Just after ten, Jayne decided to go to bed. She wouldn't achieve anything by sitting up any longer and she felt totally exhausted.

She made some cocoa and was on her way upstairs when the doorbell gave one of its intermittent jangles. It hiccuped a couple of times and then rang properly. The doorbell was yet another thing on her list of urgent things to be fixed.

But who on earth could be calling at this time of night?

She went to the door and peered through the frosted glass. The figure on the other side looked like a woman.

'Who is it?' she called.

'Me. Chloe. Come on, Jayne. It's freezing out here.'

'Chloe? What on earth . .? Why didn't you let me know you were coming?' As she spoke, Jayne struggled with the keys and managed to heave the door open.

'Oh, Chloe, come here. It's wonderful to see you.' She pulled her sister-in-law into a hug.

'I'd better get my backpack in before you close the door. I wasn't exactly sure which house it was, but Mum's description of 'a rotting pile in splendid isolation on top of a cliff' was a dead giveaway.' Chloe laughed. 'I think it's fab and can quite see why you wanted it. The decoration's a bit grim though, isn't it?'

'Nothing a few dozen tins of paint won't put right.'

Chloe came in, carrying a rucksack that had clearly seen better days. Dumping it in the hall, she began opening doors and peering into various rooms, exclaiming in delight at each one.

'Jayne, it's heaven — there's so much potential. It needs a lot of work though. But *I'm* here now. We'll start tomorrow. Good thing you're not overloaded with furniture — it'll make it much easier to do the work.'

'What do you mean, you're here now?'

'Well, I don't have any plans for the next few months, so I'll be your decorator, in return for the odd slice of toast and cheesy spread. I can't tell you how much I've missed cheesy spread, the last few years. I couldn't find it in Malaysia. What do you say? Have we got a deal? Any more of that cocoa going? The kids are in bed, I assume? I can't wait to see them — Mum says I'll never recognise them. I wouldn't mind a slice of toast right now, actually. I've been on the road since lunchtime.'

Feeling slightly shell-shocked, Jayne went into the kitchen and made fresh cocoa for them both. She stuck two slices of bread in the toaster and put a plate and knife on the table.

'How's big brother doing? I couldn't believe it when Mum told me he'd been up a ladder. I just can't imagine him doing his own house maintenance. I thought he'd have to be surgically removed from his desk to do anything manual.'

'He's coming along, but it's going to be long job. But how did you get here?'

'Hitched. I've been in London for a few weeks. Mum rang me this morning to tell me about Dan, so I slung all my stuff into a bag and here I am.'

'You hitched? All the way? Don't you know how dangerous that is?'

'I made it, didn't I?' Chloe grinned. 'You're beginning to sound like Mother, heaven forbid. She's getting worse, isn't she? She worries over nothing. She was very scathing about this place — she thinks you're making a terrible mistake. And how on earth did you persuade Dan to give up his safe practice and start again?'

'He'd had enough of the pressure of working in the city. Traffic's a nightmare, parking is impossible — and public transport never runs on time. Besides, with computers, an awful lot of work can be done at home these days. We hadn't bargained on this accident, though.'

The two women chatted on, late into the night — four years of news couldn't wait.

At last, however, Jayne knew she must go to bed or she would never be up in time for the school run next morning. There would be more time for talking in the next few days.

★   ★   ★

It was hard work persuading the children to go to school next day. They wanted to stay at home to hear all their auntie's news.

'Please stop calling me 'auntie',' Chloe protested. 'It makes me feel a hundred years old to have such a grown-up niece and nephew calling me 'auntie'. It's 'Chloe' from now on, OK? Now, I gather we're all going to visit your father this afternoon. So, go and get yourselves educated and I'll see you later.'

Giggling, Sarah and Carl climbed into the car.

Now that Chloe was here, life would be a lot more interesting. Her reputation had always intrigued them, and they knew things were going to be fun with her around.

Jayne looked at their smiling faces in the rear-view mirror.

With the doom and gloom of the last few days, she too knew that having Chloe to stay was exactly what they needed.

* * *

When Jayne returned from delivering the children, Chloe was still sitting at the kitchen table, flicking through a magazine and drinking coffee. The breakfast things still littered the place and Jayne began to tidy them into the sink.

'Jayne, come and sit down. I made a new pot of coffee. We need a meeting to discuss plans. Leave that lot till later.' Chloe waved a hand towards the dirty breakfast dishes.

'Oh, well, all right. But I mustn't waste time. The days seem to go by so quickly, and I have to prepare supper before we leave to visit Dan.'

'Supper? We haven't even finished

breakfast yet! Anyway, this isn't wasting time. This is important. We need to think out our strategy. It will be time well spent.'

They sat drinking coffee for another half an hour.

Chloe had looked into all the rooms in the house and had begun to realise the enormity of the task ahead.

'We have to be realistic about what we can tackle. We've got at least five potential rooms for letting and we need space downstairs for meals.'

'We? It sounds like you're part of all of this.'

'If you'll have me, it'll give me time to decide what I'm going to do with myself,' Chloe replied. 'This is exactly what I need — something to occupy me but without the need to make a life commitment. So, tell me what you're planning to do with the house.'

'Well, Dan needs at least one room for an office, and maybe some sort of waiting area, if he's going to practise from home,' Jayne began. 'The family needs space too, so that cuts down the space available for the bed and breakfast side of things. We do have cash to spend on the house, but we'd intended spending most of it on making the place really comfortable for ourselves and buying some decent furniture, but that's not going to happen now. We have to get the guest rooms looking good and I have to advertise as well. It's pretty late already for this year's holiday season. And there are other things I want to do. Gardening — growing our own vegetables . . . '

'Slow down. We have to prioritise. Let's make a list.'

'Chloe . . . thanks. Thanks for being here and thanks for your support. My ideas sound less hair-brained with you around.'

'Don't mention it. I've been going through a minor crisis too. I left Malaysia . . . well, let's just say a little unexpectedly. I really need something to get stuck into and this sounds perfect.'

'But I — we — won't be able to pay you much. You can see how things are.'

Chloe looked offended. 'Pay me? As if I'd take it! Just feed me and keep me warm, that's all I want. Your company will do the rest.'

Jayne turned away to look for paper and pencils and wondered what lay behind her sister-in-law's hurried departure from a job she had always claimed to love. But she knew that Chloe would talk about it when she was ready. Meantime, she was the very best possible person to have come back into their lives.

Chloe Makes Plans

There were ten bedrooms in the house, three of them little more than attic rooms. The children had claimed one of these each and the other one on that floor was going to be a sort of rumpus room, with a sofa bed for family visitors. Ideally, Jayne would like them to have a bathroom up there too, so that they were self-contained.

'I need to put in en-suites for the rooms we intend to let. Luckily, they're huge rooms so it should be manageable.'

'Oh, I don't think I'm ambitious enough to cope with plumbing!'

'No, Chloe. No plumbing. I won't even contemplate that . . . Oh, I forgot in all the excitement of your arrival — the kids have suggested a peeling party at the weekend, with everyone invited helping to strip off the old wallpaper. I've said yes, but I'm not really sure about it. What do you think?'

'Could be fun. Yes, it should work. Do you know enough people, between the lot of you?'

By the time Jayne and Chloe had sorted out a list of things needing to be done to the house, a list of people to invite to the peeling party, and a shopping list, it was almost lunchtime.

'Good gracious! At this rate, the house won't be finished until Sarah's twenty-first birthday! That's a whole precious morning wasted,' Jayne grumbled.

'Nonsense. It was time well spent — we now have a working plan,' said Chloe briskly. 'When will we phone plumbers to get estimates? What's for lunch?'

'I don't know. I don't know what's in the fridge — or any plumbers.'

'Yellow pages.'

'Chloe . . . hang on. Not yet . . . '

'We need advice, and it'll probably take days for anyone to come round, so we need to get our name down. Book a plumber and then decide on exact plans. Shall I open a tin of soup, if there is one? And cheese on toast?'

They had their simple lunch and Jayne organised something for supper in readiness for their return from the hospital.

'We'll have to leave in about half an hour so's we can collect the kids on the way to visit Dan. He'll be so surprised to see you.'

'I can't wait to see *him*,' said Chloe.

The two children were waiting outside their school, hopping around anxiously, obviously keen to see both their aunt and their father.

'Hi, kids. Had a good day?' Chloe asked.

'Not bad. Can't wait to see Dad. Hi, Mum. You OK?'

Everyone seemed to be chatting at once, and Jayne gave a little sigh as she drove towards the hospital. Dan's sister was a lively and cheerful soul who would keep them going over the coming, difficult, weeks. It was never dull when Chloe was around and Jayne was grateful for her company.

They all trooped into the huge hospital and then trudged along the seemingly miles of corridors towards Dan's ward.

'Quite a place, isn't it?' Chloe remarked. 'I wonder how many miles a day a nurse has to cover?'

'At least the wards aren't too large. Just up here and round the corner.'

'Hi, Dad. Look who we've brought to see you!' Sarah was all smiles as she held her aunt's hand.

'I don't believe it! Chloe! Where did you spring from?'

Chloe and Dan hugged each other, and then Dan looked at her properly.

'You're looking thinner than I remember. Gosh, it's good to see you. So tell me all about things. When did you arrive? Fancy me being stuck in here the first time you visit us in years. Trust me to miss out on everything.'

'Excuse me — don't I get a hug?' Jayne protested.

'And me,' Carl and Sarah added, both at the same time.

'Sorry. It's all a bit of a shock,' said Dan.

Dan was delighted when he heard that his sister was going to stay on indefinitely. But when she suggested she was going to help with the house renovations, he spluttered in disbelief.

'You are kidding! I can't imagine you with a paint brush. You'll get more on yourself than on the walls.'

An argument ensued, with Chloe protesting violently, and the children chortling with laughter.

'What made you come back to England?' Dan asked.

'Things got . . . difficult.' Chloe looked away from them all and seemed momentarily upset. 'So, here I am.' She brightened up and changed the subject immediately.

Jayne and Dan exchanged glances and Jayne shook her head, warning her husband to let the subject drop. Something had clearly upset Chloe, but she would doubtless talk about it when she was ready.

'Sea Haven is going to be the number one bed and breakfast in the whole area,' Chloe chattered away enthusiastically. 'We're having a paper-stripping weekend and a plumber's coming round by the end of the week.'

'Oh, great! We're having the party after all?' Carl said excitedly.

The remainder of the visit was spent making plans, although Jayne noticed that Dan was rather quiet, clearly feeling excluded from all the excitement. He lay back, looking very tired, and at last she decided to call it a day.

'Come on, troops, I think your dad's getting tired with all your chatter. You all go on down to the car. I just have a few things I need to talk to him about.'

Chloe took Jayne's car keys and hustled the children out.

'I'm sorry, love. It was insensitive of them to go on and on,' Jayne said quietly. 'I know that you must be feeling left out. But we do have to move on and get things done in readiness for the holiday season . . .'

'But it isn't what we planned. We were going to do it all together — make our plans together and do the work gradually.'

'I know. But if we can get things up and running with the B and B, it'll help with the finances. We have to get on with things. Make the most of what we've got.' Jayne forced herself to sound positive. 'I'll use what I need of the legacy and if we do a lot of the work ourselves, there might be some left over. Are you happy for me to go ahead, getting quotes from plumbers and planning the rooms?'

'It seems I don't really have any option,' said Dan. 'But please, let me know everything that you do. Keep me in the picture, every step of the way. I don't want to come home and not recognise the place.'

Jayne clutched his hand, realising it was going to be very difficult to keep him involved when he was so utterly helpless.

Finding time to do all the work, fetch and carry the children, and fit in long hospital visits, would mean life was going to be very complicated for the next few weeks — and she really needed Dan's support.

Their reason for buying Sea Haven, and for wanting to change their lifestyle, had been so that they could spend more time together, with Dan not working so hard and for such long hours. Her own contribution was supposed to be as his secretary, not as chief labourer restoring the house.

'It'll all be worth it in the end,' Jayne said, trying to comfort him. 'I'd better go or the kids'll be wrecking the car. I can't trust Chloe to keep them in line.'

'Its good that she's arrived to keep you company. What do you reckon was going on in Malaysia? And has she mentioned the chap she was supposed to be engaged to?'

'Alistair something or other? No.

Nothing. I expect they've broken up. She'll talk when she's ready.' Jayne stood up. 'Now I'd better be off.'

'I miss you so much. I hate being here.' Dan held on to her hand.

'Oh, Dan, I miss you too. You'll never know how much. Is there anything you need?'

'Just you.'

With a heavy heart, Jayne dragged her hand away and tried to look cheerful as she said goodbye. She turned to wave as she went out of the ward and saw him wipe away a tear. She knew that he had been trying to delay her and she felt desperately sad that she couldn't stay with him for longer. It was going to be a very long few weeks and for Dan, they'd feel even longer, she was sure.

Somehow, she had to support and sympathise with him, but still maintain the pace of progress at home as well as looking after the children.

* * *

When she got back to the car, Chloe and the children were busily engaged in making plans for the weekend.

'Right, Mum, this is the plan so far,' Sarah announced. 'We get all our friends who came to the party last week to come to the peeling party, and tell them to bring their parents. They all bring what tools they have and we divide people into teams for each room. We'll need buckets, steps and scrapers, basically, and . . . what else . . . ?'

'Hold on,' said Jayne, 'you can't *demand* that people turn up. They may have plans of their own. And there were about twenty kids here last weekend — if they all arrive with parents, I'll have to spend the entire time cooking . . . even if it is only pizzas.'

'No worries, Mum. Leave it to us. We'll sort it all,' said Carl. 'You just need to write a sort of newsletter. You can do it tonight and we'll print it off on the computer. We'll take it to school tomorrow and they'll all turn up on

Saturday. Or should we make it Sunday?'

'Saturday and then if anyone can't come the first day, they can come the second. And they might enjoy it so much they come again on Sunday,' said Sarah hopefully.

'I'm not happy about this,' Jayne said doubtfully.

'Why not?' Chloe challenged. 'I think it's a great idea.'

'Lots of people have offered to help out, however they can, while Dad's in hospital,' said Carl. 'Luke and Emily said they'd help, and so did their mum, and I bet there are loads of others who'd enjoy it.'

'I'm not sure 'enjoy' is the right word,' said Jayne wryly. 'And I'm not entirely happy about a letter going out.'

By the time they arrived back home it was getting quite dark. Supper — a casserole — was almost ready after a long slow cooking in the oven.

'Right, homework and supper. By the time I get the vegetables done, the casserole will be ready. We'll discuss any plans while we're eating. Go on — get yourselves organised.'

As soon as they had disappeared, Jayne confided her worries to Chloe.

'I don't think I can send a note to these people and ask for help. I think it might be better coming from the kids themselves, don't you? They can ask their friends and if the odd parent comes to join them, that will be great.'

'Maybe you're right. Let the kids organise it. If it's intended as a kids' event, at least they'll all have some fun. They can't do any damage, can they?'

It was agreed. The children would invite some of their friends and they would just see what happened. Chloe agreed to search out a load of pizzas and soft drinks at the supermarket, while Jayne organised the rooms and equipment they might need.

In a flash of inspiration, she collected together a bundle of chunky coloured felt pens so they could all draw pictures on the old paper before it was peeled off. It would be fun.

★   ★   ★

When she visited Dan the following afternoon, she made sure he knew all about the plans for the weekend, but she tried not to make too much of it so that he wasn't upset at missing out. It was a delicate balance.

'I left Chloe cooking supper. She was doing something exotic with vegetables and nuts. I couldn't see a recipe book anywhere, so I think she's making it up as she goes along.'

'Heaven help you all. I thought hospital food was bad but Chloe's cooking is probably ten times worse.'

Jayne laughed. It was good to hear Dan crack a joke.

'We haven't seen her in years, don't forget,' said Jayne. 'She may have learned to cook during her stay in Malaysia. She certainly seems a lot more mature than I remember her, but

I suppose that looking after others is a great way of growing up fast.

'Anyway, whatever Chloe's little faults and quirks, I have to say that she's being an absolute angel at the moment, and I really don't know what I'd have done without her — goodness, it's almost school gate time. I can't believe how quickly time whizzes by.

'I'm sorry but I'll have to go. I'll bring the mob again tomorrow, so we'll be a bit later. Thank heaven's it'll soon be Friday. Then we'll be able to relax without rushing about to do homework and to get everyone fed and watered.'

'Poor Jayne. It's all falling on you, isn't it? I'm so sorry.'

'Now don't start that again. You just concentrate on getting better. I'll have to dash. Hope you feel better tomorrow. Bye, darling.'

Dan clung to her as if he couldn't bear for her to go.

'Sorry. I just hate to see you walk

away through those doors. It always seems so final when they close behind you.'

'It's tough on the rest of us, too. We so want you home, but you have a lot of work to do to get yourself well. We're doing our best to manage without you, but I might bring the folder of household things in for you to organize. You know, the bills and stuff. You always do that.'

'Well, if you like. But I can't sit up much.'

'OK. Not to worry, it was just a thought. It's something you might have been able to help with.'

'In a few days, maybe. I don't feel up to doing much at the moment.'

As she walked away, Jayne was worried.

It hadn't taken very long, but Dan was already becoming adapted to life in the hospital. Although he wanted to feel involved in the life of his family outside, he was obviously starting to feel too detached to actively do anything, even in a simple way. It was easier to let life wash over him.

It occurred to Jane that the coming weeks were going to present even more problems than she had realised.

★　★　★

The children were excited by their plans for the weekend. It seemed that everyone they'd invited wanted to come along. Some of them said their parents would come too, as everyone was so sorry to hear about Dan's accident.

'Claire says she'll bring steps and some scraping tools,' Carl told his mother.

'Claire? When did you speak to her?'

'Outside school this afternoon. She was waiting for Luke and Emily so we asked if it was OK for them all to come.'

'You mean you asked Claire if she would come to work for us and what she could bring?'

'Yes. Why not? She's our friend, isn't she? And she didn't mind, honest. She also said she'd bring some salads for lunch, to go with the pizzas.'

'Oh, dear. This is all getting embarrassing. Who else have you asked?'

They rattled through a list of about fifteen names and claimed that everyone had said 'yes', and that most of them thought their parents would come too.

Jayne began to worry even more. At this rate she would need to spend half a day shopping, spend a small fortune, and be cooking for hours.

'Chill out, Mum. It'll all be cool. It'll be fun and nobody's being forced to do things if they don't want to. We could get the whole house cleared of all the nasty old wallpaper and be ready to paint in no time,' Sarah said, smiling happily.

★　★　★

When they arrived home, interesting smells were wafting from the kitchen.

'What's cooking?' Carl asked Chloe suspiciously.

'It's a Malaysian dish. A mixture of vegetables and nuts, and I've made a sort of sauce to go with it,' Chloe informed them.

'What's 'a sort of sauce'?' asked Sarah.

'I'm not sure yet. Depends how it turns out.'

'Dan warned me about your cooking,' Jayne said with a chuckle. 'I said you'd probably improved since school cookery classes.'

Chloe glared, and continued stirring vigorously.

'How was I expected to carry stuff home from school cookery lessons without it getting damaged? It was bound to look a mess by the time it was served. Oh, by the way, there's a plumber coming tomorrow at ten-thirty. Sounded really nice. A reliable sort of chap who seemed to know what he was talking about.'

Jayne was taken aback.

'Oh! I'd intended to get the weekend over with before I started looking for someone . . . and I'll need several estimates before I decide what to do. Well, before Dan and I decide.'

'That's what I thought. So I've arranged for another plumber to come in the afternoon and a third on Friday morning. But Mr Polglaze sounds the best. He's the one coming tomorrow morning. Names and numbers are on the pad by the phone. There's no point in putting these things off. It could be weeks before any of them can start work.'

'Oh Chloe — you're incorrigible.' Jayne smiled affectionately. 'But thanks. You're right — we do need to be ready to move as soon as possible.'

Once supper was over, and the children went off to do their homework, Jayne and Chloe sat with pads and pencils, sketching out the possibilities for the renovation of Sea Haven. It looked an extremely daunting prospect and Jayne felt sad to be making all these plans without Dan's input.

'I'm not sure how much of this is

possible,' she said to Chloe. 'To do all this would probably mean using nearly all of my uncle's legacy, and I'm beginning to wonder if we should hang on to some of it. We have no idea how long it will take before Dan's able to work again. Oh, Chloe . . . it's all a nightmare. Perhaps your mother's right — we should sell up and move into somewhere smaller.'

'No way! Think about it, Jayne — nobody's going to want a place like this unless it's in tip-top condition. You'd lose too much money if you sold it now. But if you do run it as a bed and breakfast, that'll bring in some money, won't it? And the work has to be done before you can set up in business. Come on now, let's clear up and have an early night. Or maybe there's something on television you'd enjoy? Come on, Jayne, you're a strong person — you'll get through it.'

Jayne clenched her fists determinedly. 'Of course I will. Superwoman, that's me. Sorry, Chloe — I was just having a down moment. We always make decisions together, Dan and I, that's all. It's a good job you're here to keep me going. Thanks so much for coming.'

The two women hugged each other and Jayne felt the tears pricking at the backs of her eyes. It was good to have a friend to rely on.

★   ★   ★

By the time Mr Polglaze had taken a good look around next morning, Jayne had a much clearer idea of the work that needed to be done.

Initially, if it wasn't too expensive, they would start by installing ensuites in the five bedrooms intended for letting. Once the plumbing was sorted out, they would be able to tidy up most of the rooms with the planned decorating.

Mr Polglaze was Cornish born and bred and spoke with a wonderful local accent. He was probably in his fifties, Jane thought, and she felt an instant sense of trust in the little man.

'Best if you show me round first and explain what it is you're thinking of having done. Then we can see where it's all going to fit in.'

'Right. Well, the plan is to put in en-suites in five bedrooms which I hope to be able to let out in the summer months. Depending on the estimate, of course. We do have central heating of sorts, but that might also need a bit of updating.

'Sounds sensible to me. Let's look a minute, shall we? Where do we start then?'

Jayne took him upstairs and they went from room to room, inspecting the state of the building as they went.

'Hmm . . . It's all a bit unloved, isn't it?' commented Mr Polglaze.

'I'm afraid so.' Jayne nodded in agreement. 'It's been empty for such a long time. We know it's going to take a lot of work to put the place to rights, but we've fallen in love with it.'

'Hmm . . . It's really taken it out of

the place, nobody living here for all those years. But likely you'll get it all set fair and square. Yes, I can see you've got it in you to sort it all out.'

'Well, thank you,' said Jayne, surprised at his comment. 'But it depends how much it will all cost. I'm prepared to do as much as I can myself, but clearly I'm not skilled in plumbing or electrics so I'll have to get help.'

'You'll have to have everything approved, too. Can't have guests in if you haven't got all your safety certificates. And the food hygiene people as well, I don't doubt.'

'Oh, goodness, I hadn't thought about that!'

'Well, I do have approval for plumbing and I use an excellent electrician to do the electrical side, so I'm sure we can sort it all out for you. Now, were you wanting me to do the building work as well? The divisions of the rooms, and so on?'

They chatted about his suggestions and he pointed out things that Jayne and Chloe hadn't even thought about. It certainly wasn't going to be cheap. But Mr Polglaze took away Jayne and Chloe's lists of jobs, and sketches of the rooms, and promised he would provide an estimate directly.

Jayne frowned. 'Directly' to the Cornish meant *sometime*. And more often than not it meant *sometime never*. By the time they received the estimate, and got the work underway, it would be well into the holiday season and she would be missing out on possible income.

'He's only the first of several,' Chloe reminded her.

'Yes, but I liked him. I felt he could be trusted and would do a good job.'

The next man arrived soon after lunch and they repeated the tour with him, once again describing what it was that they wanted to be done. His favourite phrase seemed to be, 'Ooh, bit ambitious that is, darlin'. Possible, but it'll cost ya.'

'I somehow doubt we'll be using that

one,' Jayne said grimly once he'd gone.

'Oooh, dunno, darlin'. It might cost ya,' Chloe said with a giggle, giving a perfect impersonation of the man.

They both laughed as they got themselves ready to collect the children and to visit Dan.

★   ★   ★

They tried to cheer up Dan by telling him about the plumbers and Chloe did her impersonation of the second man, much to the amusement of the children.

'You have to have that one,' Sarah laughed, 'just so I can see if he's as bad as you make out.'

'Any thoughts so far, Dan?' Jayne asked, seeing him looking depressed.

'It's up to you. It's your legacy and your project. I'm not much use to anyone, lying here. Do what you think's best. If I ever walk again, it'll be nice to know there's somewhere to come home to.'

80

'Hey, come on, Dad, cheer up,' Carl said. 'We'll keep you off ladders in future, but you'll be able to do most stuff, won't you?' Carl glanced at his mother for confirmation.

She nodded and smiled. 'You're just feeling a bit down, love. It's bound to happen. Have they had you out of bed yet?'

'Nope. I've just been lying here, exactly where you left me yesterday. Oh, they gave me some stretching exercises to do and I'm supposed to keep hauling myself up on this handle thing. It'll keep up the muscle tone in my upper body, so the ridiculously cheerful physiotherapist says as she breezes in and out. She's little and trim and must weigh about two stone. I'm over six feet tall and quite unable to lift myself on any handle. It feels as if the whole bed's about to collapse if I do.'

'Wicked! Go on, Dad, show us.' Carl was grinning. 'It would be cool to see you collapsing a hospital bed.'

His dad didn't take the bait. 'Not just

now. I'm too tired — must be all the pills they're giving me. In fact I think I could do with a bit of a rest. Do you mind?'

'Of course not, if that's what you want. So, I'll just go ahead and see the other plumber, shall I?'

'Whatever you want. I'm sure you'll make the right decision.'

'Cheerio for now, Dad. Hope you feel better soon. Love you,' said Sarah.

Both children gave their father hugs, to which he responded half-heartedly, and he was little more enthusiastic with his wife or sister.

'Would you prefer me to come on my own tomorrow?' Jayne asked. 'Perhaps you find all of us a bit much?'

'Sorry. I just feel angry that I messed up so badly,' Dan muttered. 'I'm missing out on everything, just lying here, useless and helpless.'

'Well, as I said yesterday, you could certainly help by doing the household accounts. When you're feeling better, I'll bring the stuff in for you. It would be a great help to me to know things were all going through properly.'

'If I must. I'll try to cheer up a bit tomorrow — promise. Thanks for coming and sorry for being so grumpy.'

They all trooped out of the little ward and Dan settled back.

He knew he shouldn't cry but a few tears forced their way from his eyes. He felt so awful as he lay back and closed his eyes. What sort of husband was he?

A useless one, he told himself.

Getting Started

The children argued all the way home, upset by the hospital visit. They felt as if their father was ignoring their feelings and had been disinterested in all their news.

'He didn't even sound pleased that I've got a rugby trial for the junior team, and he's usually so keen for us to join in with stuff,' grumbled Carl.

'And I got ten out of ten for my French vocabulary test today — and they were really difficult words,' muttered Sarah.

'Your dad's not feeling too good today, so don't take it personally,' Chloe said soothingly. 'It must be pretty boring lying there, not able to move an inch. He's usually such a busy man, isn't he? It's a bit of a shock to his system to be made helpless — especially when everything's just about

84

starting to happen at home and he's missing out on it all.'

'When did you become so perceptive?' Jayne asked her sister-in-law, with a smile.

'I've grown up since you last saw me. I've seen things that have altered my life and changed my ideas about what I want. So, who's cooking supper tonight?'

'I vote Mum does it. No offence, but I didn't much like your sauce stuff last night,' Sarah said. 'I want sausages or something.'

Chloe pulled a face. 'My talents are never appreciated. Or maybe your gourmet tastes are not yet fully developed.'

'It was a bit strange,' Jayne confirmed.

'It was more than a bit strange,' muttered Carl. 'It was blooming horrible!'

'There you go. See? Nobody appreciates me. I might as well pack right now . . .'

'No, no, no,' yelled the children in unison.

'You're fun and we haven't seen you for nearly long enough.'

'We need you.'

'Well, in that case, I might be persuaded to reconsider.'

★   ★   ★

Eleven helpers were expected on Saturday for the peeling party. Sarah had organised three of her friends, and Carl had four friends and two sets of parents.

Jayne still felt slightly embarrassed about the whole thing, but her son and daughter were adamant that everyone was enthusiastic.

During that evening, several more phone calls came through, promising more recruits, and various parents called to check that their offspring had got the details right. Jane knew some of the parents from meetings at the school, and most of them said that they would bring tools and additions to the buffet meal.

'I'm not sure how I can fit in a visit to Dan amongst all this,' said Jayne.

'If you like, and if I can borrow the car, I'll go and visit him on Saturday, and you could stay here,' offered Chloe. 'And I'll go and do the shopping tomorrow while you see the third plumber.'

'Great. That makes sense. It's probably better if I stay here with the volunteers. At least I know them slightly. Then, if I visit tomorrow, on my own, Dan won't feel as if I've put him last on my 'to do' list. Do you know what, Chloe? It looks as if some things are falling into place after all.'

'This peeling party is going to be fantastic,' Carl said cheerfully. 'I'll organise the music, and maybe we can set up some speakers to link up with all the other rooms so that everyone can hear it. Should be well wicked.'

'Where do you youngsters get these expressions?' Jayne sighed. 'What does 'well wicked' mean? And we are definitely not having your dreadful noise piped into every room. Besides, there will be parents in every room.'

'Us kids could do upstairs while the wrinklies do downstairs. Save them having to climb the stairs, poor old things.' Carl grinned cheekily.

'Do I count as a kid or a wrinkly?' asked Chloe, her eyes twinkling.

The children looked at each other and screwed up their noses as they thought about it.

'Maybe you could be an honorary kid some of the time. But I expect you'll soon revert to type and be more of an adult. Maybe not quite a wrinkly, but we'll see.'

'Well, thanks for that, I'm sure.'

★   ★   ★

After the third plumber had visited and made his suggestions, Jayne came to the conclusion that, out of the three, the only one she could rely on was Mr Polglaze.

The others may have been younger,

and possibly more up to date in their working methods, but she didn't feel comfortable with them and, more importantly, didn't entirely trust them.

So, assuming that he provided reasonable estimates for the work, Jayne would be offering the job to Mr Polglaze.

It was quite late by the time Chloe came back from her shopping expedition. The car was filled to bursting with brightly-coloured pizza boxes, bottles of soft drinks, huge bags of crisps, and carrier bags holding unidentifiable bulky packages.

'Goodness, have you bought up the whole shop?'

'Not quite, but I thought I'd better get plenty. You can always freeze what you don't need. And there were plenty of bargains on offer. I'm afraid I've spent all the money you gave me, though,' Chloe said cheerfully. 'But it's all in a good cause, and much cheaper than paying decorators to take off the old wallpaper.'

'Oh, Chloe, really! You have gone over the top. I never intended you to spend all the money. Half of that was really 'just in case' money.'

'Well, we can live on leftover pizzas for the next three weeks if we have to.'

'We might well have to. I've got to start economising somewhere. It could be weeks — months before I get any regular money coming in.'

'Sorry, Jayne. I didn't think. We'd better have something to eat now, and then you can get off to see Dan. I'll make a start on getting the rooms ready for tomorrow. Which do you think we should tackle first?'

'Take your pick. The hall needs doing, the lounge, dining-room and pretty well all of the bedrooms.'

'It's quite daunting, isn't it? But the bedrooms are empty apart from yours and the kids' rooms, so it would make sense to start with those — especially if there's building work needing to be done in them. They'll be the letting rooms and potential income. We can see what the walls are like underneath the crazy roses and mad stripes. Then they can be plastered while the rest of the work's being done.'

'Heavens, Chloe, you sound like a professional. Good thinking. I'm too swamped by the whole thing to think properly. But we need to get some of the downstairs done, too. I'm not sure people will want to stay in a house that has orange walls and purple woodwork in the hall.'

'No, you're right. So we'll strip off all the paper upstairs and try to get rid of the orange and purple down here. Have we got any paint at all?'

'Only dregs.'

'So, you'll need to call in for loads of paint on your way to visit Dan. There's a DIY place near the hospital. Buy a few gallons of white and some rollers and stuff, so that we can start to make this place habitable.'

'We were only asking people to strip off old paper, not actually decorate.'

Chloe shrugged. 'Well, some of them

might want to do a bit more. Hey, come on, cheer up, Jayne. This is going to be fun. I'll start moving any clutter and I'll cart it all up to the spare room in the attic. Then I'll see what I can find in the way of tools and things.'

Jayne felt her mind blurring under the assault of the full force of Chloe's enthusiasm. There was a huge amount of work to be done and the slow and gradual development of the rooms was becoming an urgent race against time. They needed the business to be up and running in just a few weeks.

Chloe and Jayne ate a snack lunch and then Jayne headed off to visit Dan. If she hurried, she could indeed buy a load of paint and equipment on the way to the hospital. If there were some extra willing helpers tomorrow, they could really get ahead with things.

As she drove away from the house, Jayne slowed down and looked back at it. It was a gorgeous place with wonderful views, but oh, dear, it looked so run-down and sad. She just hoped they hadn't bitten off more than they could chew, especially with this unexpected change in circumstances.

She wondered if Dan would be up to discussing finances today. He was the accountant, after all, but at the moment he seemed to have opted out of life outside the four walls of his ward.

★ ★ ★

The traffic was extremely heavy and, even without stopping for her intended purchases, Jayne was almost late arriving at the hospital

Finding a parking space was even more difficult than usual, and as she got out of the car, the heavens opened and down came the rain.

She arrived at Dan's bedside half drowned and feeling very grumpy because she'd wasted so much valuable time stuck in traffic jams getting there.

'Is it raining then?' Dan asked unnecessarily.

'You could say that. Anyway, never

mind. How are you today?'

'Oh, you know.' He sounded listless.

'No, I don't. That's why I'm asking.'

'Not brilliant. I got carted down to some sort of gym and was expected to try to haul myself around.'

'That's good. It must mean they think you're improving,' Jayne said encouragingly.

'Not really. It was just a chance for them to vent their masochistic tendencies. I was in agony, but nobody seemed to notice.'

'Poor Dan. You never were any good at being a patient.'

'This is different. I feel so helpless. And you can't believe the pain — it's a constant nagging.'

'Poor Dan. I'm really sorry. The children send their love by the way — and so does Chloe. She's being wonderful. She's really changed, and she's made some good suggestions for the house.'

'Well, that's something, I suppose. It's good to hear she's grown up at last.

Has she said any more about the reason for her hurried exit from Malaysia?'

'Not a word. She'll tell us when she's ready,' Jayne said, shrugging off her wet jacket and sitting down. 'Dan, I need to talk to you about money and the work that needs to be done on the house. I've found a plumber to install bathrooms in the rooms we need to let out, but I'm just not sure how much of our cash we should be spending at this point.'

So they sat for a while discussing their finances and, although Dan was clearly still feeling left out of things, they agreed that it made sense to start work on the work as soon as possible.

It would be money well spent because the income from bed and breakfast would not only help to keep their heads above water just now, but would be a welcome extra, even after Dan was 'back in business', as he put it.

To give herself time to buy paint before she collected the children, Jayne had to cut her visit short.

'Will I see you tomorrow?'

'Sorry, but it'll be Chloe tomorrow. I'm going to be up to my neck in pizzas, wallpaper and paint. I'll see you on Sunday with the kids. Keep working on the physio. No pain, no gain, as they say.'

'I love you, Jayne, and I'm sorry I'm such a useless misery.'

'Oh, Dan.' She leaned down and gave him a hug. He clung to her as if he would drown if he let her go.

'Dan, I must go or I'll be late for the children. Bye, love.'

* * *

The DIY store was crowded with shoppers, and Jayne hauled the trolley around, desperately trying to hurry. It seemed as if everyone in Cornwall had been bitten by the decorating bug.

She put a number of huge tubs of paint into the trolley and several packs of brushes and rollers. The house was about to be turned white throughout, she thought, as she grabbed filler and scrapers and a large pack of disposable gloves.

A glance at her watch told her she hadn't time to buy anything else.

At the checkout, someone was arguing about a special offer that hadn't shown up on the bill, and Jayne fumed as she waited, unable to do anything about it as the time ticked by.

At long last, she made it out of the store and dumped everything into the boot of the car, flinging the trolley back into the packing area.

By the time she arrived at the school, Carl and Sarah were the only two children left waiting.

'Where were you? Miss Barber came out to see if she needed to phone you, but I said you'd be at the hospital. Is Dad worse or something?' Sarah looked anxious.

'No. I've just been held up because of really heavy traffic, and I needed to shop for paint and stuff. I'm sorry you were worried.'

'We just hoped you hadn't had an

accident, too. We couldn't manage without *any* parents. And the thought of living on Chloe's cooking . . . gross!'

'Don't be so horrid, Carl,' protested Sarah. 'She does her best and she is fun to have around. Oh, no! Mum, she isn't cooking supper tonight, is she?'

'You're as bad as he is, Sarah.' Jayne laughed. 'We haven't discussed it, actually. She might well have decided to cook something by the time we get back. Judging from the amount of shopping she bought, it'll probably be pizzas tonight. And tomorrow. And possibly Sunday and for the rest of the week.'

'Sounds good to me.' Carl beamed happily.

'You should get all your homework done tonight,' Jayne suggested. 'Then you'll be free to help with the decorating over the whole weekend.'

'Oh, Mum,' chorused both children.

'Have a heart,' complained Carl. 'We've been slogging away at school all week. We can't do our homework tonight! We need a break!'

'Well, it's up to you,' said Jayne. 'But don't complain if you can't join in on Sunday, or go to see Dad.'

They arrived home to find that Chloe had been working hard. All the furniture had gone from the hall, and she'd removed the rather frayed stair carpet which the previous occupants had left behind.

'I took it out to one of the outbuildings. I didn't think you'd want to put it back — it's really tatty. You know, the outbuildings have a lot of potential, too. You could develop them into more accommodation.'

'Maybe in a hundred years. One thing at a time. One major project a week is enough for me.'

'Oh, yes. Mr Polglaze called. He wants to pop round this evening for another quick look and to check that his estimate is correct. Someone's cancelled a job and, knowing that you're anxious to get work started here, he thought he'd come round to look the place over again and to get the go-ahead from you. He's coming at seven.'

'Wow, that's fantastic. I'd already made up my mind that he was the one, if his prices were right. Oh, well, I'd better get supper ready.'

'No worries. I've got it all organised,' announced Chloe.

The children's faces fell.

'Chicken pie, jacket spuds, and fresh broccoli.'

'That sounds great,' Jayne said doubtfully. 'Doesn't it, kids? But how on earth did you find time to make a pie?'

'I didn't — it's frozen. And I can hardly spoil jacket spuds, can I? But I'll leave you to do the broccoli.'

'Oh, Chloe, come here and give me a hug.' Jayne couldn't help laughing. 'You're wonderful. You've obviously worked really hard, and you've done wonders, managing to clear the hall and stairs.'

She'd also managed to store the odd

bits and pieces from the bedrooms up in the smallest attic room, where there were still various boxes that were needing to be emptied from when they'd moved in.

'We're going to have to buy a whole load more furniture,' Jayne said as they ate. 'Maybe we can get some of those build-it-yourself things.'

'Or go to some auctions,' Chloe suggested. 'I bet there's loads of stuff you could buy at auctions in Cornwall. People upgrading hotels and such. Some nice old pieces would go well in here. We can get auction catalogues when we're ready to start looking.'

* * *

When Mr Polglaze arrived, he'd changed out of his working clothes and was wearing a slightly threadbare suit and tie

'Good evening, my dear. I hope this isn't inconvenient for you.'

'Certainly not. In fact, I'm very grateful that you've come back so quickly. My sister-in-law says you had a cancellation and might be able to start soon?'

Mr Polglaze nodded. 'The people I was going to do some work for were having a granny-flat built, but granny decided she wasn't for leaving her own place. So there you go. Just needed to check on a couple of things here, before I give you the estimate.'

'Right. Well, where would you like to start? What do you need to look at first?'

'I was thinking that if we shifted around the positioning of the ensuite bathrooms, we can make a cheaper job. Put them back to back instead of at opposite ends of the rooms. As for the heating, well, that's a bit more complicated. There's such a long run of pipework. It'll be expensive to do the whole place. It's some large old place this one, it is.'

Jayne heard the children giggling at Mr Polglaze's accent and she glared at them. Jayne loved to hear the Cornish accent, including some of the strange turns of phrase.

'So, what are you thinking would be best, then, Mr Polglaze?'

'I think you might consider some heaters, but you'd need to get some wiring work done. I know a good electrician who could do it for you.'

He went up the stairs, his feet echoing on the bare boards.

'I don't think we'll live long without a stair carpet,' Jayne remarked.

Mr Polglaze strode around the rooms, making little humphing noises and scribbling on his notepad. His suggestions regarding the placing of the bathrooms made a lot of sense.

'Right, missus. I reckon I can do all this. It'll take a week or three, but if I get my mate organised as well, we should be able to work together and get the job done how you'll like it. I'll have to get my boy to type up the estimate properly. He's good with them computer things. I can't fathom them myself.'

'Can you give me a rough idea of the figures we're looking at?'

He scribbled down a few more notes, and gave her a figure. It surprised her. It was considerably less than she'd been expecting.

'Now, you can't hold me to that, not until I've done the final calculations. But that's roughly what you're looking at. I'll get Mike working away this evening and he'll drop round tomorrow, if that's convenient.'

'Great. We're having a working party tomorrow to get this dreadful old paper stripped off. Then you'll be able to see what's underneath. I suspect there may be some plastering to be done.'

'Well, I'll quote you for the basic job and we'll see what else needs doing later.'

All Hands On Deck

When she awoke on the morning of the peeling party, Jayne was relieved to discover that it was a fine day. Coping with a lot of damp people and muddy boots would have been too much.

They had barely cleared away the breakfast things when Claire and her family arrived. They breezed in, excited, everyone talking at once.

'I've brought a few bits towards lunch. This is such a brilliant idea.'

Several more groups arrived, and before long the house rang with the sound of scrapers, children laughing, and adults arguing about the best ways to get ancient paper off walls.

Someone had brought along a sophisticated steam paper stripper, which seemed to take ages longer than a bucket of water and a sponge. The owner argued that it was doing a wonderful job, despite the really rather alarming amount of hissing and whirring it made as it fought with several layers of ancient paper.

Jayne gave up trying to organize everyone and settled for making endless cups of tea and coffee and pouring glasses of squash.

Carl and Sarah had been right. It was amazing how quickly each room was stripped, and piles of damp paper lay everywhere. Jayne fetched some black sacks, and the soggy mess was gradually cleared away.

Amazingly, all five bedrooms were finished by noon and they were ready to start on something else.

'Let's have lunch now,' she suggested. 'Then, if you really want to do some more, we could start downstairs. The lounge is a priority and then, of course, there's the hall.'

'You mean you're not keeping it just as it is?' Claire's husband, Bill, asked. 'I thought you'd decorated it specially to jar the senses and stop people from lingering there.'

Jayne giggled. 'No, I want it all white. It'll take a lot of covering but it should work — it'll lighten everywhere.'

'Let's get to it, then. You've got the paint, I see. If a couple of us start now, we should get one coat on before it gets dark.'

'You're all amazing. Thank you so much. I thought it would be months before we got anywhere with this.'

She went into the kitchen where Chloe was sitting on one of the kitchen units, staring into the eyes of a tall, blond young man who looked as if he'd stepped right out of an Australian television soap opera.

'Oh, hi. Is er . . . Chloe looking after you?' Jayne raised her eyebrows at her sister-in-law and waited for an introduction to the young man sitting in her kitchen.

'Hello, Mrs Pearson? I'm Mike Polglaze. My father asked me to drop by with his estimate.'

His accent was clearly Cornish but

less pronounced than that of his father.

Jayne smiled at him and caught Chloe's eye. This young man was every girl's dream. He looked as if he was probably in his mid-twenties, around the same age as Chloe. Jayne could see a holiday romance blossoming.

With a smile, she took the envelope he was holding and ripped it open.

'Thanks very much — this is about the same as the verbal quote. I don't think I need even bother to discuss this with my husband. I'll accept it and perhaps you'll ask your father if he can phone to sort out a starting date.'

'I think he'll be OK to start on Monday. He's dropped his quote a little as it would be to both your advantages to start right away.'

'Fantastic. I never dreamed we could get things started so soon.'

Jayne turned away as the noises out in the hallway reached something of a crescendo.

'There's no way you are climbing any stepladders to use a paint roller,' Bill was shouting at his son. 'You and the others go and finish clearing up in the last bedroom.'

'The others are mucking about. They've scribbled all over the landing walls and made a real mess.'

'Maybe I'd better go and take a look,' Jayne said anxiously. 'Thanks for the estimate, Mike, and I'll look forward to seeing your father on Monday morning. Are you still going to see Dan, Chloe? He'll think he's been deserted if you don't get off soon.'

'Oh, well . . . I suppose so.'

'And I must be going too. I'm missing some excellent waves out there.'

Chloe looked wistful 'It's ages since I went surfing. I did a bit in Malaysia.'

'Come out with us sometime. You're always welcome.'

'Really? That would be great.'

'I'll give you a call.'

Oh, to be young again, and not have any responsibilities, Jayne mused as she left them to it.

She went upstairs with Luke to inspect the mess that he'd been talking about.

Her felt pens had certainly been well used and there was a colourful display of graffiti all over the paper.

'OK, guys, I think we'd better stop now and see if that lot will come away with the paper. Take care when you're wetting it, or you'll get yourselves covered in felt pen.'

The sounds of ripping and tearing were soon heard from the landing.

They'd all made such a splendid effort and far more had been accomplished than she'd ever dared hope, so that for the first time since Dan's accident, Jayne was feeling optimistic. The plumbing and building work was going to be far less expensive than she could have hoped, even allowing for extra costs on top of the estimate.

Claire's husband Bill was making great progress with the hall, and already the orange was disappearing.

'This is only a start. The colour's

much too strong to cover in one go. But I could pop back in the morning and give it another coat if it's any help?'

'I wouldn't hear of it. You need some time to yourself — and for the family.'

'Nonsense. I've had family hanging round my neck all day. Besides, you're about to get a request from my two to stay over tonight. I heard Carl and Sarah hatching the plot a few minutes ago. Funny, they seem to think we go blind and deaf as we get older. I gather my two even smuggled sleeping bags into the car on the off chance that they'd get an invite.'

'It's fine by me.'

By the time they all fell into bed, they were totally exhausted. Even the children settled quickly, but made up for it next morning by being awake and rushing around before seven.

Jayne groaned at the sounds of a new day beginning. Though she hadn't contributed much to the actual work yesterday, she had made dozens of cups of tea and coffee and seemed to have cooked tons of pizzas.

But looking at what had been accomplished almost made her want to cry. Everyone had been so kind, and Bill and Claire were coming back to do more today. She must find something other than pizza to feed them with at lunchtime. And she'd promised to take the children to visit Dan.

She had a quick shower and began what was surely going to be another exhausting day.

'Breakfast,' she yelled up the attic stairs. 'Hurry or you'll miss it.'

'Is it pizza again?' Carl asked hopefully.

'Not this time. You'll turn into one if you eat any more. There's cereal and toast. Orange juice if you want it. Help yourselves.'

She delved into the freezer and shoved the remaining pizzas to one side. There was a pie somewhere she could put into the oven, and with some potatoes, there would be enough to feed them all. She'd have to get used to feeding lots of people, once her business had taken off.

The four children clattered into the kitchen, sounding like a dozen or more in their excitement.

'We did well yesterday, didn't we?' Carl said happily. 'I told you it was a brilliant idea.'

'I don't know how I can ever thank everyone enough.'

'There's still an awful lot of work to be done though. You've got to decorate everywhere now.'

'Tell me about it,' Jayne sighed. 'I shall be papering and painting for weeks. Still, the next part of the work is making it look exactly the way we want it, instead of having to put up with other people's ideas. I'll get some wall-paper patterns and take them in to show your dad. We can choose them together, then he'll not feel we're making all the decisions without him. After that, we'll have to think about curtains and car-pets. Heavens, it's endless.'

'It's OK, Mum. You just need a few

lists. You always feel better when you've got some lists.'

'Our mum's the same,' Emily said. 'I don't know what it is about mums but they always seem to feel better if they've got lists.'

* * *

By the afternoon, the walls of the hall and stairs were painted white, and the woodwork had all been given a first undercoat.

The house was also reasonably tidy, thanks to all the helpers.

Everyone had eaten lunch, and Claire and her family had left to go home, giving the Pearsons plenty of time to get ready to go visit Dan.

'I don't suppose anybody has actually done any homework?' Jayne asked as they drove along.

'I haven't had time. I haven't got much anyway.'

'Just as well. Well, you'll have time when we get back, and then it's an early night for everyone.'

'Where's Chloe gone this afternoon?' asked Sarah.

'I think she's gone down to the beach to watch the surfers.'

'She likes that Mike person, doesn't she?' Sarah said.

'Yes, I think she does,' Jayne replied. 'But it's not really any of our business.'

At the hospital, the children related the weekend's events to their father, and Jayne sat back, contended to listen to their chatter.

'Oh, and Chloe's got a new boyfriend. He's the son of the plumber who's coming tomorrow. The hall's all white now. Bill and one of the other dads painted it yesterday and Bill came back and finished it today. It looks really big and very clean and light,' Sarah babbled on.

'Hang on — what plumber?' Dan asked.

'The one I told you about the other day — Mr Polglaze.'

'And he's Chloe's new boyfriend?'

'No — his son came round yesterday with the estimate and Chloe took a fancy to him and went to watch him surfing today.'

'He's gorgeous, Dad. Really tall, and blond sort of stripy hair.'

'And am I allowed to see this estimate? I assume you were going to get around to mentioning it eventually,' Dan said crossly.

'I couldn't get a word in,' Jayne replied. 'Look, why don't you two go and get a drink? Is there anything you want, love?'

Dan shook his head.

'Here you are.' Jayne handed over some money to Carl and Lucy. 'Your dad and I could do with a couple of minutes to chat.'

'They're as high as kites,' she commented as they disappeared off to the hospital shop.

'Seems as if a lot's happened in a short time,' mumbled Dan.

'Everyone was marvellous. Every-where is stripped of that awful old paper, and like the children told you, Claire and Bill have made a start on the painting. And the plumber can start tomorrow. He's given us a special deal because his other job fell through. He's a sweet man, and his prices are way below what we'd thought. I hope you don't mind my accepting him without talking to you, but it seemed such a bargain. And he can start right away.'

'I'd like to have been consulted first, but I suppose I can't complain. It's all landed on you and I should be grateful that you're capable of moving on. Speaking of which, they want me to go to a special unit in Bristol. I can get some particular treatment there to help me get moving again.'

'Bristol? That'll make it difficult to visit you.'

'I wouldn't expect you to visit every day. Maybe at the weekend, but not during the week. You'd spend all day travelling. It won't be for a while yet, anyhow. They need to make sure the bones are setting correctly. I'm afraid this is going to be a very long haul.'

'Oh, my poor love. But we have to do whatever is best for you. Meanwhile, you can help me plan for Sea Haven. I thought I'd bring in some wallpaper samples and you can help me choose patterns for the rooms. I'm going to start on the lounge first, while the building work goes on upstairs.'

'Don't worry, I'm sure you'll make excellent choices. Can you actually do wallpapering? We've always had some-one in to do it before.'

'Well, I've watched how it's done. And we have lots of DIY books somewhere. It'll save loads of money if we do it ourselves. Anyhow, I'm starting on the paintwork, which will probably take me forever.'

They were interrupted by Carl and Sarah returning. Conversation reverted to the children's plans.

It all seemed surprisingly normal, as if life had been this way for ever.

Dan had got himself sorted out with library books and said he was watching a lot of television. He had his portable CD player and a selection of discs, and seemed well settled into the hospital routine. He was even beginning to enjoy hospital food.

His friends had become the various people in neighbouring beds and he knew the details of all their injuries and all about their families. He seemed almost disinterested in what was going on in the outside world and not too worried by the events at home.

'We'd better get going,' Jayne said at last. 'The kids still have homework to do. We've been so busy, it's been left to the last minute.'

'Make sure you do it properly,' Dan told them. 'Give me a hug and be good for Mum. Help her as much as you can.'

'We will. 'Bye, Dad.'

They trooped out and Dan lay back,

exhausted. He reached for his CDs, feeling glad that he had a way to cut himself off from everything. After all, if he was totally useless, he might as well lie back and try to enjoy something.

Another Disaster

When Monday morning arrived, Chloe drove the children to school while Jayne waited for Mr Polglaze.

'I've brought the catalogues for you to choose your bathroom suites while I do some measuring up,' he told Jayne when he arrived, handing her a pile of glossy brochures.

'Great, thanks — I can't wait to see it all taking shape.'

'I'll be bringing my son with me some days. He helps me when I can drag him away from the beaches. He's a surfing addict.'

'So I gather. I'm sure my sister-in-law will be delighted if he comes to help.'

'Always one for the ladies, he is. She's not here today, then?'

'She went out. Took the children to school and then stopped off to do some shopping. Seems she needed some new clothes — I can't think why.'

Jayne's eyes twinkled and Mr Polglaze laughed.

Chloe had realised that if there was to be a new man in her life, her meagre wardrobe wouldn't match up to the challenge.

Jayne left Mr Polglaze upstairs measuring for bathroom suites, and made a start on painting the lounge.

She had become quite absorbed, when the phone rang. Heaving a sigh, she peeled off the disposable gloves and went to answer it. She might not have bothered but, with Dan in hospital, she never dared ignore it.

'Jayne dear? It's Flora. You didn't ring me at the weekend to let me know how Daniel is!'

Her mother-in-law sounded even more petulant and cross than usual and Jayne's heart sank.

'There's an improvement, but it's going to take a long time,' Jayne told her. 'They're talking of sending him to a specialist unit in Bristol to help with his mobility.'

'I think I'd better come down. You'll need me to help look after the children while you're travelling so much,' declared Flora.

'That's very kind, but we're in rather a mess at the moment. We're having some building work done and everywhere is being decorated. I'd much rather you came when things are in less of a muddle.'

'But I want to see Daniel. And he will want to see me.'

Jayne bit back her retort. The last person they all wanted to see at this time was Flora. She would just fuss around, demanding constant care and attention.

'And you have Chloe staying with you, and she'll need looking after too,' Flora continued. 'Unless she's thinking of coming home soon. She was scarcely here for five minutes before she went dashing off again.'

'Chloe's been a great help,' Jayne told her. 'She's camping out in the attic rooms, with the children.'

'The attic? How dreadful! Is that the best you can do for my grandchildren?'

'It's their choice. We have five other rooms for them to choose from, but it was the attic rooms that they wanted,' Jayne said firmly. 'Look, Flora, it would be quite easy for you to speak to Dan if you want to. There are phones at the hospital. As for us, we're managing really well but there is a great deal to do. We'll invite you over as soon as possible.'

Her mother-in-law chattered on for several minutes more, expressing her disapproval of the situation.

Jayne sighed as she finally put down the phone. It would be awful to have Flora staying here while all this work was being done. She wasn't an easy guest at the best of times, but the thought of her interfering at every turn was unthinkable.

Then she felt very guilty. Of course Flora would want to see her son. She would want to reassure herself that he really was all right — Jayne was sure she would feel the same if it were Carl.

Glancing round at the chaos, however, she reaffirmed her decision to postpone any visitors for the present.

★   ★   ★

Chloe arrived back some time later in a flurry of shopping bags.

'The sales weren't quite over, so I got loads of bargains. Come and look at what I've bought. Oh, is Mr P. here? Yes, of course he is. I saw his truck. I don't suppose Mike is with him? No. I guess not.' The whole speech was made with barely a pause for breath.

'Where do you get your energy?' Jayne asked her. 'You just missed speaking to your mother on the phone. She wants to know when you're going home. She misses you.'

'You didn't say I'd go, did you?' Chloe asked in alarm.

'Of course not. I wouldn't make plans for you. I said you were being useful here — some of the time,' Jayne teased. 'So, she wants to come down here, as an alternative.'

'You're kidding! Mum and this lot simply won't work. She'll drive us all bonkers.'

'I know. That's why I said we'll be delighted to see her when things are a little less hectic.

'Can I get on now? I'll see your bargains when I stop for lunch. Perhaps you can organise that? Then I can finish painting this skirting board.'

'Lunch is organised already! I bought some goodies in the market for lunch treats. Half an hour?'

Jayne sighed. Getting the house finished was going to take for ever if this was going to be typical of her day's work. Collecting the kids from school, and then visiting Dan, took up all her afternoon, and the mornings seemed to be one hold-up after the other.

If truth be told, if Dan *was* moved to Bristol, that would release quite a lot of time. She'd miss seeing him, of course, but it was so difficult to fit everything in.

'Chloe, you couldn't do me a favour, could you? Could you pick up the kids and go visit Dan this afternoon?'

'Sure, no problem,' agreed Chloe.

Great. That would leave Jayne at home to get on with the painting. It also meant she would be around to make any decisions regarding the bathrooms and to organise Mr Polglaze.

He'd been very quiet upstairs and had accepted several cups of tea and coffee when offered but otherwise seemed engrossed in his measurements and planning.

'I could leave you a kettle and things up here if you like,' Jayne had suggested to him. 'Then you can make drinks whenever you like.'

'Very good of you, missus. Kind thought.'

'Please call me Jayne, Mr Polglaze.'

'George,' he replied. 'I'm George.'

'Good. That's settled. And I hope you won't mind working in the house alone when I'm out. I have to visit the hospital most days.'

★ ★ ★

The next week didn't see a great deal of progress, although yards and yards of piping was delivered, and the landing gradually disappeared under piles of shower trays, lavatory bowls and hand basins.

Mr Polglaze seemed to be making a huge mess everywhere.

In due course, boxes of fittings and taps joined the mound of stuff on the landing, but none of this vast array of plumbing equipment seemed actually to be getting installed anywhere.

'He has to get the pipes sorted out before he can start to fit anything, I expect,' Jayne said hopefully to the children and Chloe, but she was beginning to lose patience. After the great start, everything seemed to have slowed right down.

A load of wood had now turned up,

along with a number of large sheets of fibre board, and it had all gone to form a brand new heap on the landing.

'That's going to be used to separate the rooms, I expect,' Carl said, nodding wisely. 'I've seen it used on those television make-over programmes.'

The collection of plumbing and building supplies grew every day.

George Polglaze smiled happily at each new delivery.

'We'll soon have everything looking shipshape. Things are coming on a treat,' he said on Friday evening. 'We did a good deal with the wholesaler, buying so much at one go. Saves us a bit of money. We'll be seeing you on Monday sharpish.'

'Right,' Jayne said doubtfully. 'Is it all right if we put some of the stuff into one of the rooms? It's a bit tricky to move around up here.'

'That'll be all right.' He nodded. 'Oh, and I can put you in touch with someone to paint the outside of the house. He'll do a proper job and won't charge too much. I'll tell him what's what.'

'That would be great. I'm not going to tackle anything that involves high ladders.'

'Right you are, missus. I'll send William round right soon.'

'Thanks.' She waved to him as he drove away.

'Well, it looks as if that's it for now,' Jayne said to Sarah. 'Maybe I could go and look at wallpaper tomorrow and take a break from painting. I feel as if the paintbrush is surgically attached to my arm.'

'You've done well, Mum. I really like all the white paintwork in the hallway. It makes it look much brighter. What colour are you going to do the living-room?' Sarah was looking around the lounge, which seemed huge without furniture and carpets. The rather elderly three-piece suite was stacked in the dining-room, along with the rest of the lounge furniture.

They discussed colour schemes, and

Jayne dreamily described the room she'd been hoping for. The walls would be a soft buttery yellow, with a carpet of similar shade. She'd also seen some curtains, gold with red flowers and swirls.

'And then I'd have a darker red suite, maybe with flecks of gold again, and cushions in shades of red and gold, too. I saw the scheme in a magazine.'

'But what will you really have?' Sarah asked.

'I expect it will be green on the walls and a neutral carpet, because we have to make do with the old suite.'

'I think we should go with your idea. It would look lovely.'

'Too expensive, I'm afraid. No, I have to be sensible. But it's nice to dream a little.'

'Where's Chloe gone?' asked Carl, looking sulky and bored.

'I'm not sure. I think she may have gone out with Mike again.'

'She's getting really boring lately, isn't she?' Carl complained. 'Always mooning over Mike.'

'Don't exaggerate. She's not always mooning over him. Besides, she's an adult — she can choose what she does with her own life.'

'Three nights running. Are they going to get married?'

'Oh, for goodness' sake, Carl. They're just spending some time together. I don't suppose for a moment that it's serious. She'll probably go back to . . . well, she'll probably be back off on her travels before long.'

George's friend William had arrived and was making short work of painting the outside woodwork. He'd even fixed the broken guttering that had been the start and the cause of all their problems.

Looked at from the outside, the whole place had been transformed from a derelict looking mess to a cared-for home.

Towards the end of the following week, most of the dividing partitions had been put up, and George was almost ready to begin tiling.

It seemed he was a master of most trades, and he worked on steadily, gradually completing his tasks.

It was while Jayne was downstairs in the lounge, discovering that wallpapering wasn't quite as easy as it looked, that she heard a great crash and a yell.

'Oh no,' she muttered and ran out of the room into the hallway.

'George? Mr Polglaze? Are you all right?'

Silence. Even the banging had stopped.

She ran up the stairs, dreading what she might find.

She found him lying on the ground, a jumble of strips of wood and the steps on top of him. Jayne went cold. It was almost a repeat of Dan's accident. Mr Polglaze had blood pouring out of a cut on his cheek and was lying twisted round most unnaturally.

'Oh, George, whatever happened?'

'Slipped a bit I reckon. I'm sorry, missus. I think I've damaged my arm.

Oh dear, oh dear. This is going make working a bit tricky.'

'I'd better call an ambulance. You'll need an X-ray on your arm and they'll have to check that there isn't anything else wrong. Will I call your son? Or your wife?'

'You'd best call Mike. He's got one of them mobile things. He can come and take me to hospital and drive the truck home. I don't want an ambulance coming. I expect he'll be out in the waves though. Oh dear, oh dear.'

'I'm beginning to think this place has a curse on it. First Dan and now you.'

Jayne dialled the number that George Polglaze had given her, and was relieved when Mike answered straight away.

Waiting for Mike to come for his father, Jayne pressed a pad of tissues against George's bleeding cheek and tried to make him comfortable.

George straightened up gingerly, and it seemed there was no major damage apart from his arm.

Mike arrived very shortly after Jayne

had called him, and drove his father to the hospital.

After they'd gone, Jayne put the kettle on and sat down heavily. She felt exhausted and frustrated. If George had broken his arm, he'd be unable to work for weeks.

★   ★   ★

It was late in the evening that the phone rang and her fears were confirmed.

'Mrs Pearson? It's Mike Polglaze. I'm afraid Dad's broken his arm. I'm really sorry, but he's not going to be able to work for a while.'

'I thought that would be the case. How is he? Any other injuries?'

'A few cuts and bruises. And severely damaged pride — that's probably the worst of his injuries.'

'Well, wish him all the best, but I'll have to see if there's anyone else we can get to help. I don't suppose you know of anyone?'

'There's me.'

'You? Can you do this sort of work?'

'Well, I'm used to helping Dad out, and the work's all pretty straightforward really. And the electricians are booked, aren't they? If I carry on where Dad left off it would save any hold-ups in the work.'

'Well, if you think you can do it, thanks very much. I was dreading the thought of having to try to find someone else.'

'I'll be round first thing.'

'Fine. Give my best wishes to your father and wish him a speedy recovery.'

Jayne felt incredibly weary as she hung up.

'Oh, Dan,' she muttered. 'I really need you. I'm just not strong enough to do all this on my own.'

The phone rang again and when she answered, a slightly muffled voice asked to speak to Chloe.

'Who is this?' she asked.

'Is Chloe there or not?' the voice demanded angrily.

'Tell me who's calling and I'll see if

she can speak to you.'

'Tell her to call me. Tell her I need to speak to her. She'll know who it is.' The phone was slammed down at the other end.

'Now what on earth was all that about?' Jayne wondered, alarmed.

★   ★   ★

Mike turned up promptly at eight o'clock the next morning and started work immediately. He refused the endless cups of tea and coffee favoured by his father, and was soon fixing the large sheets of fibre board to the frames that George had built. He had a radio with him and whistled cheerfully as he worked. His pace seemed quite a lot faster than his father's and the progress he was making was impressive.

Chloe watched him devotedly and lost interest in helping with either the decorating or fetching and carrying the children.

'Perhaps you could paint some of the

woodwork around the bedrooms,' Jayne suggested.

'Not much point. The wood shavings will stick to the wet paint. Anyhow, I'm going to help Mike do the tiling next.'

'You are?'

Chloe nodded happily. She was on a high again after sinking low last night when she'd heard about the mysterious phone call. It was quite obvious that she knew who it was but she'd refused to say anything. Jayne was concerned, but there was nothing she could do.

'We've agreed that my dad will come round to supervise some of the plumbing work, just to make sure everything's as it should be,' Mike told Jayne. 'Tiling's something I can do without his help, and it will be easier to do it before I attach the various bits to the wall. Saves cutting round the fittings, and I can drill through the tiles to fix the bowls and everything.'

'That makes sense. OK, I'll leave you to it and get back to my decorating. Chloe, I'll let you organize coffees?'

Jayne went downstairs, sighing. It looked as if she'd get very little help from her sister-in-law while Mike was around.

As she continued to develop new skills with wallpaper and paste, Jayne thought about the coming holiday season. Easter was only a few weeks away and, if she was to maximise any income from a bed and breakfast business, she would need to advertise.

Originally, Dan had talked of using the Internet and a website, but Jayne knew little about any of that, so that idea would have to go on the back burner.

Perhaps she could advertise in local newspapers? And she might get passing trade through cards in shops, but meantime she needed some advance bookings from holidaymakers living outside Cornwall.

She would need to organise it very soon, and she made up her mind to talk to Dan about it that afternoon. The phone interrupted her thoughts.

'I need to speak to Chloe,' the same gruff voice from yesterday announced.

'Who's calling, please?'

'She knows. Just get her.'

Jayne called upstairs and Chloe came to the top and stood silently shaking her head. She was flapping her hands and mouthing '*No*'.

Jayne stared at her and held out the phone gesturing '*Yes*', but Chloe retreated back into the bedroom. Helplessly, Jayne spoke into the phone again.

'I'm sorry. She must have gone out. Where did you get this number?'

But there was silence, and the phone was put down at the other end.

Jayne hung up and went angrily up the stairs.

'Chloe, this has got to stop. Who is it calling you? You can't avoid them for ever. For goodness' sake, you must tell me what's going on.'

'I'm not going to talk about it. I'm sorry, but you just have to say I'm not here — I've gone away. Now, please drop the subject. Mike, shall I spread the cement stuff over here?'

Fuming, Jayne went back downstairs. Why was Chloe being so mysterious?

This person who kept on phoning didn't sound very nice. Threatening somehow, and sinister. What could be going on, and why wouldn't her sister-in-law speak to him?

All too soon, it was lunchtime, and the end of Jayne's chance to complete her tasks for the day. It looked as if she would have to work at night if the room was ever going to be finished. She had hoped that Chloe would help to hang the paper, but that clearly wasn't going to happen while Mike was in the house. Still, if it meant the tiling was completed a little faster, Chloe helping Mike might not be a bad thing. It might make his job a little more pleasant, too. The thought of putting up acres of white tiles must be daunting to even the best worker.

Once again, Jayne had gone for white everywhere as it didn't date, and she planned to add splashes of colour with towels and accessories. She had also chosen off-white for the floor tiles, and would put down large washable fluffy bath mats, to make everything as easy as possible. She looked forward to shopping for all the extra goodies that would make the place homely and welcoming.

As soon as lunch was over, Jayne went to visit Dan, leaving Chloe and Mike still working. They'd completed two of the bathrooms already, so they at least were getting on well with the work, and that particular part of the job would soon be nearing completion.

★　★　★

'I reckon we're going to be ready to decorate the bedrooms by next week. Amazing isn't it?' Jayne told Dan excitedly. 'Then we need to think about advertising. Have you any ideas?'

'Not especially. You can't really go with the website idea on your own, can you? Maybe you could advertise in the local paper?'

He seemed totally unenthusiastic and detached.

'I'm being sent to Bristol next week. I have to do exercise without any weight bearing and it seems I can't do that here. Seems crazy to me, but there it is. Can you bring in some clothes for me? I need tracksuits, so you'll probably have to buy some.'

'Well, that's good news. It must mean you're making progress. I know it won't be nice for you to miss seeing us all, but perhaps it won't be for long.'

'A couple of weeks, then it's back here for another week, and then I should be able to come home.'

'Wow! That's great. At least we have a timetable to work from. If you work hard at it, maybe you'll be able to come home sooner.'

'That might not be convenient for you with all your plans,' he said peevishly.

'Oh, Dan, don't be silly. I'm only

pushing ahead with everything because of the uncertainty over money. We need an income and it may be some time before you can earn again. It may seem rash spending our ready cash the way we are, but at least it'll bring something back in. What do they say? Speculate to accumulate.'

'Whatever. I'm just a useless burden to you.'

'Please, Dan. I know you're depressed, but it doesn't help me to hear you talking like this. Let's talk about something else. Oh, yes — Chloe's mysterious caller. There's someone trying to phone her — a man. He won't say who he is and she does everything possible to avoid him.'

'That's worrying. What's she been up to, I wonder? Is it an English caller?'

'I don't know. You can't really tell where the call comes from.'

'Have you tried dialling one-four-seven-one?'

'I didn't think of that. I will next time, if he calls again.'

She hoped she hadn't given her husband yet another thing to worry about, but at least the change of subject had worked and he'd stopped wallowing in self-pity.

Poor Dan. He must be finding all this so difficult. They'd always done everything together. Decisions and work had always been shared, and now she was doing it all.

As she drove to collect the children, she thought once more of how much more time she would have available once Dan was in Bristol, and immediately felt very guilty.

★　★　★

'We're back, Chloe,' she called, when she arrived home with the kids.

Strangely, the doors were locked and Mike's truck had gone from the drive. It was only four-thirty and rather early for him to have left. The house was silent.

Jayne went upstairs to see what

progress had been made, but there didn't seem to have been any more work done since she'd left after lunch.

She hoped nothing had gone wrong. She couldn't cope with any more dramas.

She sighed, and went to prepare supper while the children did their homework.

It was almost seven by the time Chloe returned, glowing from being out in the fresh air, and with damp hair.

'What a fantastic afternoon! I've never enjoyed the sea so much. Mike's been giving me surfing lessons. I even managed to stand up on the board!'

'Are you telling me that you and Mike have spent the whole afternoon surfing?' Jayne was aghast.

'Yes, it was fantastic. The waves were perfect.'

'How nice for you. So the work was abandoned while you and The Hunk cleared off to the beach?'

'Chill out, Jayne.' Chloe gave a tinkling laugh. 'You've been working too hard. You should try surfing. It's the greatest buzz.'

'Of course I'm working too hard!' Jayne exploded. 'Perhaps you've forgotten the pressure I'm under to get everything done before the visitors start to arrive?'

'Well, I'm sorry.' Chloe looked angry. 'But I've been working, too,, you know. And I'm not exactly getting paid.'

Jayne sighed. 'I'm sorry, Chloe. Of course you're entitled to enjoy yourself. But not to take my worker away with you. Mike has a job to do.'

'Only because of his good nature,' Chloe pointed out. 'He offered to help you and his father out, but he doesn't have to, you know.'

'OK. I'm sorry. Maybe I over-reacted.' Jayne slumped sadly in a chair. 'Dan was in a bad mood this afternoon and I just feel grumpy too, now. He's going to Bristol next week and is feeling depressed about it. Anyway, come on, we'd better eat — the kids'll be starving.'

Things Get Better!

During the following week, the electricians arrived and completed the wiring jobs incredibly quickly. There was certainly something to be said for local knowledge, Jayne realized. Without George's influence, she knew it would have been a much longer job. They had been expensive, but the new storage heaters seemed to be clean and efficient.

Mike worked very hard each morning but seemed to disappear any afternoon when the surf was good. He had an uncanny knack of knowing exactly when that was, and Chloe usually disappeared with him.

Chloe also took to bringing Mike back to share the evening meal, which concerned Jayne slightly as she felt obliged to make a bit more of an effort, which cost more time, money and effort.

It all led to more tension in the household, but Jayne said nothing.

At last, the final stages were approaching and Jayne was able to plan the finishing touches to the rooms.

She was becoming much more adept at papering now, and had bought enough rolls to do the bedrooms. Each bedroom was to be a different colour, to allow for easy identification when the time came to let them.

George was coming in each day to supervise his son as the bathroom fixtures were fitted, and Jayne was papering and painting along behind them as they went.

Soon, all five rooms were nearly done. It was time to think about carpets, curtains and furniture.

'Try that store down by the harbour in Trillian — cheapest stuff in the area and good quality with it,' suggested George. 'And there's always the auction rooms.'

Jayne began to make her plans, calculating that all the work would be completed by the next day, so she should order carpets and organize someone to come and fit them as soon as possible.

'There are just the doors to put on now, and then we'll be finished. Shall we go and see what the surf's doing, Chloe?' Mike suggested.

Chloe looked at Jayne uncertainly.

'Go on,' Jayne said, smiling. 'So long as it's all finished tomorrow. And then you can come to the shops with me and help choose carpet.'

'Cool. Surf today — carpets tomorrow. What more could a girl want?'

The pair rushed off, hand in hand, and Jayne watched them with a smile. She and Dan had been like that once, she remembered, and suddenly she felt quite old.

'Oh, Dan,' she murmured, 'hurry home. I do so miss you.'

She sat down in one of the almost completed bedrooms and felt sorry for herself for a while. But she didn't allow herself to mope for long, for what was the point of that? Wearily she hauled herself to her feet and began the usual rounds of preparing supper and collecting the children.

It seemed so long since she'd had time to do anything for herself. In another few days, Dan would be back from Bristol and she would have to start the daily visits to him again. It seemed so selfish to grumble about that, but those few days when she'd been able to work through the whole day had made such a difference.

She was actually becoming a very competent decorator, she thought, proudly. But after the last few weeks, she'd be pleased if she never had to hold a paint-brush again.

Chloe hadn't returned from the beach by the time supper was ready, so Jayne and the children sat down to eat and left her food to keep warm. If Mike came back with her, they would have to share what there was, Jayne thought grimly. As no arrangements had been made, it was too bad if there wasn't enough food.

'Chloe's no fun any more, is she, Mum?' Carl said as they finished. 'She's always mooning over Mike. I wish Dad was back.'

'He soon will be, love. We could phone him later and see how he's doing, if you like?'

'But he's not very interested in us either, is he?' Sarah put in.

Jayne bit her lip guiltily. The children were right. Everything had changed.

'Things will come right again. It just takes time,' she assured Carl and Sarah. 'Hey, guess what? Chloe and I are going to order the carpets tomorrow — and buy new curtains — and we're going to look at some auction catalogues.'

'Thrilling,' said Carl, in a very bored voice.

'We'll be able to advertise our rooms and get lots of bed and breakfast guests to help pay all the bills.'

'That means you'll have even less time to spare,' Sarah moaned. She got up from the table and left the room.

Carl looked miserable, too. 'I'll go up and do my homework,' he mumbled, and followed his sister.

Jayne felt tears welling up. But there was nothing she could do. They all needed to face up to the truth that things were not going to be easy, at least not for the foreseeable future.

She cleared the supper things and got out her lists.

It was time to move on.

★　★　★

Chloe arrived home just as it was getting dark.

'Oh good,' she said breezily, 'I was hoping you wouldn't wait for me for supper.'

'Tough on the kids if we'd waited till now.'

'Sorry. We stopped at the pub and Mike treated me to a bar meal. The surf was fabulous today. I'm really getting quite good — I can stand up on the board quite well now.'

'Well, good for you. Your supper's keeping hot — in fact, it's probably dried to nothing. You could have said you weren't coming back, Chloe. I can't afford to waste food.'

Chloe sat down beside her. 'What's up, Jayne? You sound really stressed.'

'I *am* really stressed. I'm tired. I'm missing Dan. I have no idea what's waiting round the corner. And the kids keep growing so fast I can hardly provide clothes that fit them for longer than five minutes.'

'Oh, poor you! Come on — let's open a bottle of wine and cheer you up.'

'Can't afford it.' Jayne snuffled.

'Oh dear, you really *are* feeling sorry for yourself! Shopping for carpets and stuff may help you. If Mike finishes work on the upstairs tomorrow, as he thinks he will, we can go shopping the next day. At least you'll soon see some results after all your hard work.

'We're going to make this the most popular B and B in Cornwall! It's time we sorted out some adverts. Can I use the computer? I reckon I could put some sort of website together. We'll borrow Mike's camera and take some pictures of the area. Some good surfing shots. In fact, Mike probably has some already.'

'But the house is still a mess!' Jayne protested. 'We can hardly show what the rooms are like.'

'In a day or two they'll be looking wonderful. Mike's dad says there's an auction in Truro on Tuesday. We'll go and buy loads of everything we need.'

Jayne was cheered by Chloe's enthusiasm and they spent the evening working on their ideas for advertising and also planned the shopping trip.

'Thanks, Chloe, and I'm sorry I was so upset,' Jayne said, as they were heading for bed.

'I'm sorry too, Jayne. I've been thoughtless, and I was so caught up in the excitement of learning to surf and being with Mike that I was forgetting why it is I'm really here. To help you and Dan,' she added.

'You really like Mike, don't you?' Jayne pressed.

'Yes, I really do like Mike. I like him a lot. He's fun and exciting. And easy-going. It makes such a nice change after all the . . . ' Abruptly she halted.

'After all the what?'

'Oh, nothing. Just thinking aloud.'

'Is it something to do with your hasty retreat from Malaysia?'

'I don't want to talk about it.'

'Is your mysterious caller something to do with that as well?'

'Oh, Jayne, don't — you really don't want to know any of this.'

'OK. It's up to you, Chloe, but it might help you to talk.'

'No, that's the last thing I want. It's all behind me. All over and done with. Now, do we have any cocoa? That's what we both need right now.'

★ ★ ★

The two women wandered around the massive carpet store, clutching notes of measurements and pieces of wallpaper, trying to match colours.

'I don't know where to start,' Jayne wailed. 'There's too much choice. I don't want colours that are too light as they'll show the dirt — and dark colours are murder to clean, too. They show every speck of fluff. I think I'll have to go for one of these textured ones. They won't show the dirt, will they?'

'No idea — carpets aren't really my thing,' Chloe said apologetically. 'Are we getting the same everywhere? Or different colours for each room?'

A salesman stepped forward and offered to help.

After several minutes of discussion, he showed them the special offer of the week, telling them that if they bought enough of it to carpet all five bedrooms, they could have a reduction of ten per cent on the already discounted price.

'But it's *beige*,' Chloe wailed. 'It'll look so boring.'

'But ten per cent off,' Jayne said. 'It'll save a fortune.'

'But if you hate it, you'll want to change it sooner. You're buying for the long term here and you'll regret it if you don't get exactly what you want. Why don't we go for something to tie in with the dominant colours in the paper?'

Chloe led Jayne through the maze of giant rolls and showed her a selection of tweedy textures in pastel colours.

'See? If you get these, then you can add more colour with bedding.'

'Well, it'll cost more, but . . . '

'Leave it with me, Jayne. You just wait there and I'll sort this out.'

Chloe dashed off and Jayne could see her arguing with the salesman. They were nodding and gesturing and then he abruptly walked away and left Chloe standing there.

A few minutes later, he returned, smiling. Jayne wondered what was going on.

'Right,' said Chloe, returning to her side. 'If we buy enough from this range for all the rooms at once, they'll let you have ten per cent off the total. How's that?'

'That's great. I don't know how you swung it, but let's do it.'

'And that nice red and gold colour scheme that you had in mind for the lounge? I've seen just the thing — and there's exactly the right colour for the hall, stairs and landing, too.'

'I was going to make do for the lounge, and do the stairs later.'

'Nonsense. You can't let anyone sit in the lounge with that old carpet, and the clatter on the stairs will drive everyone potty. Come on.'

Jayne felt embarrassed as her sister-in-law continued to strike deals and demand bargains right, left and centre. She even negotiated a special price for fitting.

'Good gracious, Chloe, your bargaining skills are quite something,' Jayne said with a laugh. 'I'd never have dared ask for all those discounts and a deal on fitting as well.'

'It's the charity worker's mentality. If you don't ask for stuff, you don't get it.

And the more you ask for, the more you get. There's no use being half-hearted about it.'

'Well, thanks. I'm amazed we got everything for such a reasonable price. Mind you, it's still quite a lot to spend.'

'But we're back on track, aren't we?' said Chloe. 'There's just the auction to go to, and we'll be ready for business.'

★   ★   ★

Jayne and the children visited Dan twice over the weekend, but they scarcely saw Chloe at all. She arrived home late each evening, glowing with the sun and the wind and the mysterious ingredient provided by getting to know an attractive man.

Jayne and Chloe chatted over cocoa late on the Sunday evening.

'Oh, Jayne, he's so different from any of the other men I've known. He's fun and gorgeous and seems happy to be with me. How good is that?'

'Well, I'm glad you're enjoying

yourself. Mike does seem a really nice guy. He doesn't work for his dad full-time, though, does he?'

'No. He's studying architecture. Helping his dad helps to pay for his fees. He's got two more years to go and then he'll be qualified and making big money. He's got some ideas for your outbuildings, by the way. He says he'd like to run them past you sometime.'

'That's interesting, but quite impossible at the moment. Maybe sometime in the future. By the way, I've got some news for you!' said Jane. 'Dan's being allowed to come home next weekend — just to see how we cope for a couple of days. We're getting a visit from the occupational therapist to see what equipment we'll need to look after him.'

'Oh, Jayne, that's terrific. You must be thrilled. And Dan will be over the moon.'

'We both are. I can't wait. But I guess I'm slightly apprehensive. It will be a lot to cope with.'

'Yes, but it's good that the carpet

men are coming tomorrow. At least the house will be pretty much shipshape for his visit. It was lucky the carpet fitters had a cancellation, otherwise they wouldn't have been able to put the carpets down so quickly.'

'We're doing well on other people's cancellations. And the price is all down to your cheek. But yes, it's great. I hope they finish putting all the carpets down tomorrow so we're free to go to the auction on Tuesday.'

'I'm sure they will. And Mike says he'll borrow his dad's van and trailer and come with us, so we can bring back the stuff we buy and won't have to pay for delivery.'

'Chloe, you're terrific!'

'I know. Great, isn't it?'

They hugged each other, and Jayne felt tears rising. She would never have managed without Dan's sister being so helpful and cheerful. She really hoped things would work out for Chloe with Mike.

'I'd better get to bed now. I've an

early start tomorrow.'

'Jayne, I'll do all the running around tomorrow. And I'll go to see Dan. I feel guilty that I haven't been for a while. That way, you'll be free to make endless cups of tea for our team of trusty carpet fitters.'

'OK. If you don't mind, that will be great. You're not seeing Mike, tomorrow?'

'He's got college work to catch up on. He's fallen behind over the last few weeks and his tutor is making all sorts of dire threats. The fact that he's been doing the practical work is all that's stopped him being thrown off the course.'

'That's terrible. Why didn't he say?'

'I expect he just wanted to get the job done.'

'And all those days he went off surfing?'

Chloe grinned. 'Everyone needs some chill-time, Jayne.'

Success — And A Shock!

It was quite late in the evening before the team of carpet layers left. They had worked hard and, to Jayne's delight, had managed to completely fit the entire house.

Next day, as arranged, Jayne dropped the children off at school and then went on to meet Chloe and Mike at the auction rooms.

'There's masses of really good stuff,' Chloe said excitedly. 'Whole rooms full of useful furniture.'

'Mike, it's really good of you to help us out,' said Jayne. 'I'm beginning to wonder what on earth I'd do without you!'

'Don't mention it. But I'm afraid I'll have to leave you to your own devices for a while — I have a lecture this morning. But Chloe's going to phone me later when you've finished bidding and I'll come back, load the trailer, and deliver the stuff back home for you. Good luck.'

He leaned over and kissed Chloe, then turned to wave as he strode off.

'Now that looked like quite a kiss,' Jayne teased. 'It's getting quite serious between you two, isn't it?'

'Getting there,' Chloe replied, with a blush. 'Now, shall we decide what to bid for? I hope you've brought plenty of cash.'

'I called in at the bank on my way here. Just don't get carried away and wave your arms when you shouldn't.'

'Don't be daft. It isn't that simple.'

They walked around and marked the catalogue with several items they wanted to bid for. One of the local hotels was being refurbished, so there was plenty to choose from. There was a lot of furniture that would perfectly suit Sea Haven. And, because their lots weren't coming up until later, there was time to watch and see how the system worked.

'I feel quite nervous,' Jayne confessed.

'There's nothing to it. Just keep your cool and don't worry about losing the odd item. There's plenty more to choose from.'

'I suppose so. Oh, look at that bureau. Isn't it hideous?'

Chloe nodded in agreement.

'No more bids? Once. Twice. Three times. Sold to the lady in blue.'

The auctioneer nodded towards them and Chloe turned to look behind her. There was nobody else in the area wearing blue.

'Oh, Chloe! What have you done? I think you've bought that monstrosity of a desk!'

'No. I can't have done! I only nodded at you. How much was it anyhow?'

'I dread to think. I warned you to be careful!'

'Would it fit in Dan's office?' Chloe suggested hopefully.

Jayne grimaced. 'Dan would go ballistic if he had to work with that.'

'OK. Don't worry. I'll get Mike to drive me straight to an antiques shop after the auction so's I can sell it . . . We might even turn a profit.'

'Chloe, just stand still and don't move a muscle. The first bedroom suite that we're interested in is next.'

But the bedroom suite went for much more money than they had decided to pay. Another came up and this also realised a high price.

'Oh, dear, this isn't looking good.'

'Don't worry, there are loads more bedroom suites. Even if the best ones go for more than we can afford, there's still plenty of decent stuff left that we can polish up, or even paint if it's a bit scruffy.'

'You and whose army? Don't forget, it's time itself that we're short of if we're to be in business for Easter. It's less than a couple of weeks away. Oh, look, I like this stuff that's coming up for sale next.'

Jayne put up her hand and made her first bid.

The price rose until she decided that was enough.

However, to her delight, nobody else bid any more; she now owned the double bed, dressing table and wardrobe.

Encouraged by her success, she bid on several more lots and soon had almost everything she needed.

'This is exciting, isn't it?' she said to Chloe.

'It certainly is. Why don't we get some extra chairs and some of the lampshades? And one of those boxes of pictures might be nice. There are some pretty Cornish scenes. It you don't like the pictures, we can always print off some photographs on the computer to put in the frames.'

It was almost two o'clock by the time they had finished.

'I've forgotten what we've bought,' Jayne said, worried. 'I just hope I have enough cash for it all. I've to pay for your wonderful bureau as well as everything else, remember.'

'I promise I'll get the money back. We did rather well though, didn't we?'

Jayne went to the clerk to sort out payment, while Chloe went to call Mike.

At the collection point, there was a mass of furniture and boxes awaiting them, and when Mike arrived, the van and trailer suddenly looked much smaller than they had done that morning. It was going to take at least two trips to get everything in, Jayne thought, worrying about the time and how long it would take.

They began by loading the van. Mike was clever at packing and managed to fit in far more than Jayne had expected.

'Hang on — what's this lot?' she asked, picking up a cardboard box filled with picture frames and assorted junk.

'Ah,' Chloe murmured. 'I guess that was another accident. Remember how I suggested that old pictures might be a help in filling in the wall spaces? Well, I think I must have bought some!'

Jayne looked down at her list of

purchases and grinned.

'You spent a whole fifty pence on this lot of rubbish.'

'Dock it from my wages,' laughed Chloe.

'And four pounds on the hideous bureau.'

'You'll be on the breadline this week,' said Mike, laughing. 'Oh, well, I think it's my turn to feed you! I'd better take you out for supper one night.'

'You're on,' Chloe and Jayne both said at once.

They packed everything they could into the van and trailer and stuffed the rest into the car. Miraculously, by cleverly putting things inside each other, they managed to squeeze everything in.

'We'll go and get this lot home and start unloading,' Mike said. 'Where do you want it all put?'

'Just dump what you can in the hall, and we'll sort through it and clean it up as we go. Then it needs to go upstairs.'

⋆   ⋆   ⋆

When the children arrived home from school, they were delighted to rummage through the boxes, helping to stick colour-coded labels on the various items, with different colours for each room.

After all the hard work, Jayne had a sense of the project reaching an end. All five of the new guest-rooms now had a bedroom suite with a double or single bed.

All that remained to be bought was bedding.

'Why on earth did you buy this jug? It's awful,' Carl exclaimed as he held up an extremely ugly and garishly-coloured object.

'It was just in the box as part of the job-lot,' explained Jayne. 'Don't be rude about it — it might be worth a fortune! You know what they say on that antiques programme — sometimes there are real bargains in these job-lots. Chloe's going round the antiques shops tomorrow. She may come back with a fist-full of money.'

'You're coming too,' Chloe insisted. 'You'll add an air of respectability to the proceedings.'

'Oh, I'm coming with you all right!' laughed Jayne. 'It'll be fun watching you and your bargaining skills. Now, who feels strong enough to help me carry some of this stuff upstairs?'

It was after eleven before they'd finished moving everything upstairs and had arranged the rooms.

They'd shared a Chinese takeaway with Mike and a friend of his — who went by the name of Spike — who had come along to lend a hand.

Everyone had worked hard and now the job was done. Jayne looked around the house before she fell wearily into bed.

'It's really looking great, isn't it?' she commented to Chloe.

'Brilliant. You'd never know that some of this stuff was quite as second-hand as it is. I can't believe hotel owners can afford to restock their rooms and get rid of their old furniture so cheaply. You've done a great job. Dan will be blown away by it all.'

'If he can be bothered to look,' Jayne replied. 'He isn't showing much interest in anything at the moment.'

'I noticed that. He's been away too long,' Chloe said seriously. 'He's becoming institutionalised. It's good that he's coming home this weekend.'

★ ★ ★

The trip around the antiques shops had to be postponed because Jayne had a phone call from the occupational therapist, wanting to pay her a visit that morning.

She arrived soon after breakfast and wandered round the house frowning.

'I don't think your husband will be able to manage these stairs. I hadn't realised your house was quite so large. Is there any chance of him having a bed down here? And what about a shower? Is there a bathroom downstairs?'

'Just a toilet and washbasin — no shower.'

'I think we may be able to help with installing one.'

'It all sounds very complicated for just a weekend at home.'

'I'm thinking much longer term. He'll need support for several months yet. Perhaps this room along here could be used as his bedroom?'

'That was going to be his office and waiting-room. He's an accountant and plans to work from home.'

'Then perhaps you can use the dining-room for his office instead?'

'Oh, dear. We planned to use that for our guests — we're starting a bed and breakfast business. I can see that this is going to be quite a problem. We'll get a bed down here for the weekend, and he'll just have to manage with the toilet and washbasin until we can get the shower installed.'

★ ★ ★

After the occupational therapist had left, Jayne sat down feeling quite

174

depressed. She was so disappointed that Dan wouldn't be able to get upstairs to see the new rooms — she had wanted him to share her excitement. She hadn't realised there were going to be quite so many difficulties.

'Come on,' Chloe encouraged her. 'It's no use going all mopey. We'll get there, don't worry about it. Let's go and make our fortunes selling antiques.'

'Hardly antiques. Somebody's old cast-offs, more like. But you're right, it's better than moping.'

They stowed everything in the car, even managing to fit the bureau in.

'I've got a list of places from the phone book. I thought we'd start with Truro and hope to convince the more up-market shops that we're offering them bargains.'

The first shop had a very superior lady receptionist who snootily told them that what they were offering was certainly not in her area of expertise and suggested a market stall was more suitable. Jayne cringed at her words and decided they should forget the whole idea and go home.

'Nonsense. Just because that toffee-nosed woman didn't want our stuff, doesn't mean she can spot a bargain. We'll move on to the next shop.'

They finally struck gold in one of the shops specialising in pottery.

'Do you know what this jug is?' asked one man.

'Possibly Moorcroft?' suggested Chloe, and Jayne's jaw dropped. Where had that come from?

'You may be right. The mark is rather unclear but it certainly could be one of their seconds. Sometimes flawed items did escape the net and were bought by collectors. Not so valuable as perfect, you understand?'

'Well, clearly not. But still of some value?' encouraged Chloe.

'It could be by Charlotte Rhead. It's her style, certainly. I'd like to do some research, if you wouldn't mind. Can you leave it with me for a few hours? I'll give you a receipt for it, of course, and then we'll see if we can agree a price.'

'I think we can do that, don't you, Jayne?' Chloe was trying to smother a grin.

'Well,' Jayne said, pretending to consider, 'I suppose so — providing you give us a receipt.'

When they got out of the shop, both of them burst out laughing.

'Where did Moorcroft come from?' Jayne asked. 'You know nothing about pottery.'

'I saw a poster on the wall and it looked sort of similar. Could be worth quite a bit.'

'So long as it's more than fifty pence, we're in profit.'

'Come on, let's have some lunch to celebrate.'

'We haven't sold it yet. And nobody's bought that lovely bureau, either.'

They eventually managed to offload most of their things for varying amounts of money, even the bureau, which was finally sold for fifteen pounds, much to Chloe's disgust.

'I'd have got at least twenty if you hadn't settled so easily for fifteen.'

'I wanted to be sure we got rid of it. Besides, we've only just got time to go back to the Moorcroft man before the kids get out of school.'

'The days just aren't long enough, are they?' Chloe moaned.

The dealer was grinning all over his face when they returned to his shop.

'I've checked a few details and it's almost certainly a Charlotte Rhead. I don't even think it's a second — just slightly damaged through lack of care. Now, I can make you an offer right away or you can research a bit more. You might consider a London auction for it?'

'How much are *you* offering?' Chloe asked.

As he named it, Jayne gasped. The figure was almost as much as they'd spent in total at the auction.

'We'll take it,' she said. 'If you can make a profit on it in London, good luck to you.'

'Hang on,' Chloe protested. 'Round it up to the next hundred and it's yours.'

The dealer rubbed his chin and looked thoughtful. 'Settle for the price and I'll give you an extra ten per cent of anything I make on it.'

'That sounds fair,' Jayne agreed.

They collected the children and laughed and sang all the way home.

'Oh, heavens, we didn't go to see Dan!' Jayne suddenly exclaimed in horror. 'How could I have forgotten him?'

'Don't worry about it. You haven't missed a day before now.'

Jayne phoned Dan straight away to apologise, but he seemed to understand and not to mind too much.

Jayne and Chloe spent a happier evening than they had for some time. Mike had arrived after supper to ask about their day, and he'd brought a bottle of wine with him so they were able to celebrate in style.

Presently Jayne left Chloe and Mike

to be on their own and went up to bed. The pair were certainly enjoying each other's company; she sensed romance in the air!

★ ★ ★

When Friday arrived, they were more or less ready for Dan's home visit. Mike had helped them to carry one of the new single beds downstairs to the dining-room. That way, Dan would feel part of the family instead of being shut away in what was to have been the office. Since it was only for a weekend, they had decided he would have to manage with the cloakroom.

He arrived with crutches and a borrowed wheelchair in case he needed it. He was exhausted by the time he was seated in the lounge and the hospital staff had left.

'Wow,' he said wearily. 'You've made such a difference in here. It's really nice. Yes, I like it. And the hall looks much bigger, too. Clean and light. But, oh, my gosh, I'm tired.'

'Do you want a cup of tea? Or coffee?' Jayne offered. 'What can I get you?'

'I need a good sleep, actually. But it's nice to be home — not that I recognise much.'

'Shall I leave you for a while, then? You can go to bed if you want to.'

'Sorry. The journey seemed endless, and I didn't sleep much last night either. I suppose I was excited to be coming home. I'll just close my eyes here for a few minutes and I'm sure I'll soon feel better.'

'OK. I'll leave you the little bell to ring if you want anything.'

Jayne left him and sat in the kitchen to drink her coffee alone. It seemed such an anti-climax after all these weeks. She'd been bursting with excitement at her husband's return, and now it had all gone a bit flat.

She'd hardly taken a sip of her coffee before she heard the little bell tinkling, and she rushed through to the dining-room to see what the problem was.

'Sorry, darling, but I need some help. I have to go to the bathroom. I tried to stand up and it was . . . well, impossible.' Dan sighed. 'Maybe I'll have to sit in a higher chair. Or the wretched wheelchair.'

Together, struggling, they managed to get Dan to his feet. Once up, he was able to move reasonably well on his crutches, and he made his way carefully to the cloakroom. His feet did drag on the carpets, which the occupational therapist had said they would, but at least he made it without falling. Jayne bit her lip. This was going to be a trying weekend.

But the whole family pulled together and they managed to make the most of the weekend, playing Scrabble and Monopoly and watching several old movies on television.

Jayne wasn't sure if Dan enjoyed himself or not. He kept saying how good it was to be home, but seemed not to mind too much when the ambulance came to take him back to hospital on

Monday morning.

'I'll soon be back to normal,' he promised. 'I'll work really hard to get my mobility back. I'm sorry that I couldn't get upstairs to see the results of all your hard work. But, if you're ready for it, maybe you should start advertising for guests. It'll soon be Easter and there'll be people around, looking for accommodation. It would be good practice for the summer months.'

Jayne agreed that this was a good idea, and she and Chloe went out and about, putting adverts in all the local shops.

All they needed to do now was buy extra bedding and crockery and then they would be ready for action. Excited at the thought of another auction, and possible bargains, Jayne and Chloe set off early the next day, with Jayne threatening Chloe with all sorts of punishment if she bid for more rubbish, however tempting it may be. They would never again be so lucky as they had been with the Moorcroft jug.

However, they did manage to buy several lots of bedding and a couple of boxes of china and cutlery, all at a very reasonable price.

'We'll have to launder everything and some of it may be useless, but at least it was cheap,' Jayne said happily. 'I just hope the washing machine and tumble dryer don't break down. I really can't see myself managing to trail to the nearest launderette every time I do a wash.'

'Any reason why the washing machine and tumble dryer *should* break down?' Chloe wondered.

'Of course not — I'm just being pessimistic,' Jayne admitted. 'I'm feeling quite nervous now we're almost ready for visitors. I'm not sure what people will expect.'

'A decent breakfast and comfortable beds. That's about it, really.'

'Tea and coffee in their rooms. I'll have to buy kettles and those little packs of coffee and sugar and little milk pots. I need a list . . . '

Chloe laughed and shook her head. 'You and your lists!'

★ ★ ★

A couple of days before Easter, someone phoned to ask for a room for the weekend, filling Jayne with excitement. She rushed around making sure everything was in order, checking and rechecking the room until everyone began teasing her.

'It isn't the Royal family who're coming, Mum,' Sarah laughed.

'It's got to be right, though. If someone enjoys their stay, they'll recommend us to their friends.'

The Harrisons seemed a very pleasant middle-aged couple, who were regular visitors to the area. Jayne took some homemade scones to their room, showed them the tea making-facilities, and generally made them welcome.

'Enjoy your stay, and if there's anything more you need, please ask.'

185

'Thank you, dearie. Lovely room. I'm sure we'll be very happy here.

'Is there a television we can watch? We don't like to miss our soaps.'

'You can use the TV in the lounge, if you like.'

'Thanks, lovie. We'll be down at half-past five. Is there somewhere we can get a bite to eat later?'

Jayne hesitated. Should she offer them a meal? But no, it was hardly fair on the children, and she hadn't advertised evening meals.

'There's a pub in the village where they do good bar food if that's what you want.'

'Just as long as it's nice home cooking. That's all we ask, isn't it, love? Then we'll be back for the evening episodes.'

'Fine.' Jayne smiled. This wasn't quite what she had expected. Maybe she would have to provide televisions in the bedrooms. Did bed and breakfast guests usually spend every evening in the house? She hadn't thought so.

By the end of the evening, Jayne, Chloe and the children were thoroughly fed-up. They'd gone into the lounge to find that the Harrisons were dominating the room and had taken total control of the family television.

The family were sitting together in the kitchen, complaining.

'Why do they come away on holiday if they only want to stay in and watch the telly?' asked Carl reasonably enough.

'They're only here for one night, then they're moving on.'

'It's a lot of work for only one night,' Chloe remarked.

'Maybe, but we have to start somewhere.'

Next morning, nervous about making a good impression, Jayne provided a full breakfast and put a basket of fruit on the sideboard, along with a selection of cereals and fruit juices. Their guests finally finished breakfast at ten o'clock, having had two pots of tea and more slices of toast than Jayne would have believed possible.

'Lovely, dearie,' said Mrs Harrison as they paid their bill. 'Very nice spot. We shall certainly recommend you to our friends.'

'Thank you. I'm glad you enjoyed your stay. We'll look forward to seeing you again sometime.'

'Oh, we'll be back. Not many places offer such generous hospitality.'

When Jayne went back into the dining-room to clear up, she was horrified to find that all the left-over food had been taken! All four pots of yoghurt, the entire contents of the fruit basket, and all of the little pots of preserves she'd left to give them a choice. Even the butter pats had all been used. Nobody could have eaten all that at one sitting!

She hurried up to the room, to check that all the towels were still there! They were, but all the coffee and tea packs, along with all the milks and sugars, had gone. The kettle was still warm, so she assumed the Harrisons had filled a thermos flask.

It all seemed so mean and greedy. They'd clearly taken all the extras to feed them for lunch.

'I think I made them too welcome,' she moaned to Chloe. 'I didn't realise people would take advantage like that. Well, I've learned one lesson. Limit the choices and put out only one of anything. If they want something different, they'll have to ask — and I'm not letting anyone take over our television again. I might buy the odd second-hand one for one or two of the rooms, but we're not a four-star hotel. Bed and breakfast is what we advertise, and that's what they'll get.'

'Good for you,' Chloe said, applauding. 'What greedy people! But you did make some profit, didn't you?'

'Well, yes, but the margins are small and I can't afford to give stuff away like that. They had an enormous breakfast as well.'

'Move on, Jayne,' Chloe advised.

'Learn from the experience and move on.'

'You're right,' Jayne agreed, sighing. 'Now, I'd better go and strip the beds and wash the towels.'

Bad News From School

'They've suggested I try coming home for a whole week,' Dan announced when Jayne arrived at the hospital later that day. 'I'll have to come in for physiotherapy most days, but it'll be great to be home again. I thought maybe I could use the office as a bedroom?'

'I haven't decorated it yet, but maybe I can get round to it over the next few days,' said Jayne.

'Don't bother about decorating it. Just get someone to help you put a bed in there and I'll be fine. It'll be great to feel a part of the family again. I seem to have been on the outside for so long.'

'Oh, Dan, it'll be fantastic to have you back properly. It's been so hard trying to make decisions without you.'

'And such a lot of hard work — you've been amazing.'

She only had a few days to get everything organised. To her surprise, the hospital arranged for a plumber to come and install a shower unit in the downstairs cloakroom. It was a small room but, with careful planning, everything was fitted in. There were rails added to make it safe for Dan, by giving him something to hold on to.

Jayne didn't have time to re-decorate the office as a bedroom but, with fresh curtains and the new bedding, it looked welcoming enough. She kept the room clear of extra furniture, to give Dan space to move around and to use the wheelchair if he needed it. Even though he had to return to hospital for further assessment, it felt as though he really was coming home at last.

Coping with guests and Dan presented a few problems but, after her first experiences, things had become much more stable and Jayne was more organised.

But, as yet, Jayne wasn't really making any money from the bed and breakfast business — at least, not enough to give any real security. It was an erratic way to earn a living and couldn't be relied on to bring in enough cash for major expenses.

'I feel really bad about spending all that money on the house,' Jayne admitted to Dan one evening after supper. 'If I'd waited until you were well enough to start earning again, we might not have needed to touch Uncle Joseph's legacy. Oh Dan, have I been stupid?'

'Of course you haven't. I'm going to be in and out of hospital for a good many more weeks. We're not even sure if I'm going to function properly again. Yes, we could have used Uncle Joseph's legacy to live on, but once that money had gone, we wouldn't have been able to do the work on the house . . . ' He gripped her hand. 'What you've done and are doing to keep the home going is little short of a miracle, and I can't thank you enough. And I can't wait to see what you've done upstairs.'

'You sound much more like your old

self. It's been ages since I heard you take an interest in anything.'

'I think it must be the mind-set you get into in hospital. You go into a sort of shut-down mode and the thought of things going on outside your own little world are too remote and too painful. If you didn't feel that way, I think you'd go mad wondering what was happening. I can't believe some of the things I was talking about to people in neighbouring beds.'

'It's great having you back with us now, even if it's only for a few days.'

Perhaps Dan was more like his old self again, but now it was Carl and Sarah who were both being difficult. They seemed to be having trouble adapting to their new way of life, catering for holiday visitors.

Sarah did nothing but sulk. 'You'll be glad when we're back at school. It'll give you more time to look after boring holidaymakers.'

'Please, Sarah,' Jayne appealed. 'Try to make the best of things. It isn't my fault all this has happened . . . '

'We have to share this rubbish house with all the world and his wife. It's hideous having strangers here all the time! Having to behave and be quiet. It's ruined our lives!'

Jayne closed her eyes as she felt tears pushing behind them. It had been the 'coolest house ever' only a few short weeks ago.

She swallowed hard.

'I have to take your father to the hospital for his treatment. You can come if you like and I'll drop you in town to do some shopping. Or would you rather stay here with Chloe?'

'I'm staying here — I want to make the most of it while there are no stupid strangers around.'

Jayne left without another word, slamming the door behind her.

★   ★   ★

It seemed to take most of the day for Dan to be given his treatment. They had removed the plaster casts from his legs and were using removable splints so that he could go into the hydro-therapy pool. Then there were other exercises that kept him busy for what seemed like hours.

By the time he was ready to leave, he was quite exhausted, while Jayne was frustrated at having wasted so much time, but it was too far to go home and then return to collect him. If this was to happen every day, there seemed little point in Dan being at home.

She voiced the thought to him as they drove home.

'It's only for a few more days, then I'm back in hospital anyway,' Dan said. 'We'll skip tomorrow's treatment — it really doesn't matter.'

'No, we can't do that,' she protested. 'I was really thinking of the children. They haven't got much more holiday left and it's been dreadful for them all these weeks. They're pretty grumpy at the moment anyway.'

It wasn't a pleasant end to the

holidays. The children were barely speaking to either parent. Chloe was rarely to be seen as she was always off somewhere with Mike. Jayne was stressed with looking after Dan, taking him to the hospital, and trying to answer enquiries about accommodation. She scarcely knew what to do first each morning.

At last the holiday was over and Dan was back in hospital. But his visit had been successful on the whole.

Jayne saw her two sulky children off to school on the first day of the new term, comforting herself with the thought that they would soon be complaining about their teachers as much as their parents.

When she got back home after doing the school run, Mike and Chloe were sitting in the kitchen.

'I've just made coffee. Do you want some?' Chloe offered.

'Sounds good. Do you have time off, Mike?'

'Just taking a breather — I've been

working like mad all holiday,' he said. 'Errm . . . we were talking about your accommodation problems. Chloe was telling me that Dan's having to use the room that was to have been an office, and I was thinking that one of the barns would make a perfect office. Why don't I draw up some plans for you? There's masses of space out there, and even if you wanted to develop more of it later, the nearest one would be perfect for when Dan starts his business.'

'That's very kind of you, but we've spent all our money on the house,' said Jayne sadly. 'We can't afford to do any more renovations just now.'

'I wouldn't charge. It would be a part of my course work. It's always better to work on a proper development rather than something imagined. It's a whole lot easier. I'd really like to do it, if you've no objections.'

'Well, of course not. Thank you.' Jayne was genuinely touched by his offer. 'That's really good of you, Mike. You've already done so much . . . '

'I'd like to draw up plans for the rest of the outbuildings, too, if that's OK. They'd make wonderful starter homes for young people.'

'Are you trying to tell me something here?' Jayne asked, startled.

'Of course not,' Chloe said, blushing furiously. 'Though I wouldn't mind living in Cornwall if I could find permanent work.'

They chatted for almost an hour, and Jayne finally dragged herself to her feet. There was a whole heap of washing to be done and rooms to be cleaned.

She worried about the children and hoped that being back at school might make them feel their lives were returning to some sort of normality. She decided she would make them one of their favourites for tea and hoped it would help their mood.

Jayne unloaded the washer, folded sheets and took them up to the airing cupboard. She was keeping one room ready all the time, just in case anyone turned up unexpectedly.

Her heart lifted as she went into her new rooms. Her favourite was the blue room, with the pale blue carpet and creamy wallpaper with blue flecks. The sea view was reflected into the room, and anyone who had stayed there always made the comment that it seemed like a part of the décor. She carried on with her cleaning with renewed determination. Things would come right. She would make it happen. And Mike's idea of converting the barn into an office was a good one.

Her positive mood remained with her throughout the day, despite the children still being sulky and uncommunicative when they came home.

Chloe arrived back just as Jayne was dishing up the meal. Mike was with her.

'Hi, everyone. You don't mind if Mike joins us, do you? You always have enough to feed an army. How was the first day back, kidlets?'

'Same old boring stuff,' grumbled Sarah.

'Everything's boring just now,' agreed

Carl, pulling a face.

Jayne raised her eyes to heaven and decided to ignore them. She served the meat, cutting it into slightly smaller pieces to make it go round.

'I hope you don't mind me joining you,' Mike said.

'It's fine, Mike. Really. I'd have done extra vegetables if I'd known, but we can share what there is.' She couldn't help feeling slightly irritated that Chloe could be so thoughtless — she knew they were on a limited budget! She really must have a word with her after Mike had left.

* * *

As the summer term wore on, the change in the children became obvious. They grew noticeably lazy and home-work was neglected. When Jayne was called in to a parents' evening, she was most disappointed to discover that both of them had fallen behind with their course work.

'We've always had high hopes for both Carl and Sarah,' said the head teacher. 'But now they're scarcely keeping up with their respective classes. Is there some reason you can suggest? I understand you've had problems at home? I don't mean to be personal but I really want to discover the reason for this deterioration.'

Jayne sighed. 'My husband's in hospital. He had an accident and it's going to be a long haul until he's fit again. I've been trying to build up a bed and breakfast business to bring in some income, and we've just had extensive work done to the house. It's been a very stressful time.

'I think there have just been too many changes in their lives recently, with the move here, my husband's accident and everything. And I've probably been too busy to realise just how bad things had got. I'll try to put things right — spend more time with them and try to help them more.'

Jayne felt even more guilty as she

drove home. She felt that she was jeopardising their children's whole future. She even shed a few tears and once more asked herself whether she'd done the right thing.

It might have been better if they'd never moved or had such grandiose plans. Dan's mother had been right. If he'd stayed in his old job and they hadn't tried to buy their dream home, everything would have stayed on course. She would have continued to meet friends for nice little lunches and spent days at a time wandering round the shops . . . and been thoroughly bored and unfulfilled.

As she turned into the drive and looked up at the delightful old house, she knew deep inside that they had done the right thing. It was just unfortunate that Dan's accident had happened.

'Right, you two,' she said as she walked in. 'We need to have a talk.'

'What's the old bat been saying?' Carl demanded.

'Carl! This attitude stops right now. I won't have it. I know you've had it tough, and a lot of things have happened that we never expected, but everything we did was for this family. Just a few months ago, you said this was the 'coolest house ever'.'

'It was. But you've done it up so it isn't any more!'

'We can't even go into some of the rooms in case we make a mess,' Sarah whined.

'I know that. But this is the situation that exists now and we have to make the best of it.'

They talked for some time and finally agreed that everyone would try to spend more time together, and that there would be a proper routine for homework. Any guests that came would be fitted into their family routine.

'It's half term next week, and I have at least three rooms booked already, so we'll have to try hard to make it all work.'

The children went to bed, and Jayne

slumped down in front of the television, feeling totally exhausted. There was no sign of Chloe. Out with Mike again, she supposed.

She was almost falling asleep when the phone rang. It was Dan's mother, Flora.

'Hello, dear. How's Daniel?'

'He's getting on,' Jayne replied wearily. 'He's been home a couple of times but needs rather a lot of physiotherapy, so he's staying in hospital for a few more weeks, with just the odd visit home to see how he can cope.'

'I did wonder. I haven't heard from you for so long.'

'I'm sorry. It's all been very difficult. Getting the house straight and visiting the hospital every day has been a bit of a nightmare. But things are improving now. We've had a few guests and I have several bookings.'

'Well, dear, that's why I'm calling. It's half term next week, isn't it? I thought I'd come down and see you all, and give you a hand. I've booked the train and will arrive on Saturday at four. Don't worry about getting anything in specially. I'll just fit in with whatever you're doing. Is Chloe still with you? It's very thoughtless of her, imposing like that.'

'Chloe's been great. She's worked very hard and been most supportive,' Jayne said firmly.

'That doesn't sound like Chloe. Did her friend find her? He called here several times, so I gave him your number. He said he was a friend from Malaysia.'

Jayne frowned. She'd forgotten all about the mysterious caller. He must surely have given up trying to contact Chloe.

Meantime, a visit from her mother-in-law was the last thing Jayne needed, but perhaps she was being unfair. Flora always meant well and she must be lonely living on her own.

'Right, one of us will collect you from the station. Can you book to Pengellis? It's much nearer.'

'I've already booked to Truro. That's not a problem, is it?'

'No, of course not. You can call in to see Dan on your way here. It may be Chloe who collects you as I have guests arriving during the afternoon.'

'Oh, but Chloe's such a reckless driver. Can't you do it?'

'We'll see. Goodbye then. See you on Saturday.'

Good job we've got all the rooms done, Jayne thought. And it's a blessing they weren't all booked. She'll live in luxury compared to what it once was!

Wearily she pulled out her notepad and began to make some new lists. She wrote a note for Chloe and left it on the kitchen table. She was too tired to wait up any longer for her.

★ ★ ★

When Saturday came, Chloe was annoyed that she'd been asked to collect her mother and to visit Dan.

'I was going surfing. There's a big

competition this weekend and Mike's competing. I wanted to watch — I promised I'd be there to support him.'

'Well, I'm sorry, but I have to see the guests in. Come on, Chloe, be reasonable. Your mother wants to see you as well as Dan,' Jayne protested. 'Please help me with this. I just haven't got the time to drive to Truro, look after the children, *and* organise visitors.'

'I'll take the children with me to the beach,' announced Chloe. 'They'll love it. That'll be one thing less for you to think about.'

Finally Jayne lost her temper and positively shouted at Chloe, saying it was time that she took some responsibility and stopped treating Sea Haven as a free hotel, swanning in and out without a care in the world.

Her sister-in-law looked shocked.

'I'm sorry you feel that way. I'll move out immediately. I can get a job and some digs in the village,' she muttered.

Jayne was instantly sorry. 'There's no need for that. I'm sorry. I'm just sick of having to cope with everything, and your mother isn't the easiest of people to get on with — she needs a lot of attention. She thinks she's coming to help but it'll be worse than having another guest.' She paused. 'I'm sorry, Chloe. It is your mother I'm talking about.'

'It's all right. I know exactly what you mean,' said Chloe. 'And maybe I have been taking you for granted. Of course I'll do the fetching and carrying.'

'She mentioned your mysterious caller, by the way. She said he'd called her several times and she'd given him this number. That explains how he knew where to find you.'

Chloe looked anxious. 'I'd hoped it had all gone away,' she muttered.

'Are you going to tell me what it's all about?'

'No. It's nothing. Now, shall I help you wash the sheets?'

★   ★   ★

The Saturday of half-term was wet. It was disappointing to think that Flora was going to see their new house for the first time through the swish of windscreen wipers.

It also meant that everyone would be trailing in and out with wet feet and probably wanting to hang around the house a lot more.

After that first disastrous visit from the Harrisons, they hadn't opened their lounge to guests again. Jayne had bought a couple of portable televisions for the bedrooms, and this seemed to have worked out well, though it did mean she'd need to buy more if there were several guests staying. The various requirements seemed endless. No sooner had she sorted out one thing than something else cropped up.

Chloe set off to collect her mother and to visit Dan, and left Jayne busy fussing over the guest-rooms. The children were up in the attic rooms, evidently quite happy to entertain themselves.

When the first visitors arrived, Jayne served them tea and scones in the dining-room, before showing them up to their room. She had put a pack of local tourist information sheets in each room, and her guests were soon back downstairs, asking about a number of tourist sites.

'We shall enjoy visiting the various gardens,' they said. 'We're both keen gardeners.'

'I love gardening too,' said Jayne. 'We haven't had much time to do ours since we moved here, but I hope to get around to it quite soon.'

'I hope you don't mind if we come back early? We're planning an early night after our long journey.'

'That's fine. Make yourselves at home and please ask if there's anything you need.'

They drove away, in search of gardens, and Jayne sighed her first sigh of relief.

The next group of visitors, four of them — two lots of friends — arrived at four-thirty. Jayne went through the usual meeting and greeting routine with them, and was outside on the drive giving them directions to a local beauty spot when Flora arrived with an assortment of bags, boxes and suitcases.

'Hello, dear,' Flora called as she was extricating herself from the car. 'Oh, how do you do?' she called, insisting on shaking hands with each of the confused looking guests. 'This is my son's house, you know. He's an accountant.'

Jayne's heart sank. Any moment, the entire life history of the family would be poured out to the strangers. She stepped forward hastily.

'Flora! Come on in out of this damp air. Had a good journey?' Jayne took her arm and led her into the hall, leaving Chloe to struggle in with the luggage.

'I say, this is all rather nice, isn't it? A little cold maybe, all this white paint, but fresh looking. Yes, very fresh looking. Be such a lot for you to keep clean though. Dirty fingermarks every-where.'

'I'll call the children down. Go on through to the lounge. I'll make some tea and be with you in a minute.'

Jayne ran up the stairs to the attic.

'Granny's here,' she announced. 'Come and see her.'

There were some scuffling noises and a hoot of laughter and Carl and Lucy came bursting out of their attic rooms and galloped down the stairs.

'Well, you two seem a bit more cheerful,' commented Jayne.

'A whole week off school makes anyone feel cheerful.'

Jayne felt very weary by the end of the evening, having listened to Flora as she pointed out the vast number of mistakes that had been made in choosing wallpaper, paint, bedding, furniture, and the house itself.

And, of course, it was pointed out to Jayne, several times, that poor Daniel would never have had the accident if they hadn't pursued this hair-brained scheme. Jayne was being handed all the blame, and none of the credit.

After supper, Flora wanted to know why Chloe was so anxious to go out 'I expect there's a man involved, is there?'

'I believe Chloe does have a boy-friend,' said Jayne vaguely and abruptly changed the subject. 'How do you like your en-suite? Nice to have your own bathroom and not have to share with the family, isn't it?'

'Well, yes, though I usually have a bath rather than a shower.'

'You can always use our bathroom if you prefer. We're rather pleased with the way it's all turned out. It's been a lot of hard work, but worth it.'

'If it's what you want, that's lovely for you. But I don't think I'd like to share my home with strangers.'

'We haven't much choice. Now, would you like a hot drink, cocoa or something, before bed?'

This was going to be a hard week, Jayne realised. She wasn't sure she could cope with the continual criticism.

Life With Flora

Flora was up early and came bustling into the kitchen, insisting that she would cook breakfast for everyone.

'I wouldn't dream of it,' said Jayne. 'You're our guest. I've got the coffee on, so just make yourself comfortable and I'll pour some for you.'

'I'd prefer tea if it isn't any trouble. Coffee gives me indigestion.'

Jayne made a pot of tea and set it down next to her mother-in-law.

Then she began to organize the cooked breakfasts and put several slices of bread into the large toaster.

'Here we go — I can hear someone coming downstairs. Excuse me, Flora.'

It was the group of four friends who were first down for breakfast. They all ordered a full English breakfast and Jayne left them helping themselves to cereal while she went to start the cooking. Flora insisted on helping but was more of a hindrance, always seeming to be exactly where Jayne needed to be, getting under her feet and in the way.

'Why don't you fry the sausages?' Flora asked.

'They cook themselves in the oven and it means I don't have to watch them or keep turning them over. I'll just take the coffee through. Can you keep on eye on the bacon for me?'

By the time all the guests had finished breakfast, Jayne felt utterly drained. The constant barrage of criticism from Flora, and the number of times she was asked 'why do you do this or that' had left her mind reeling.

At last, she escaped to the dining-room to clear the table. As she made her way back to the kitchen with a stacked tray, Flora was coming out and they narrowly avoided a collision.

'That was all quite fun, wasn't it?' Flora said happily. 'I'm glad I could be of help. Now, shall I bring all the bits and pieces through?' She began to gather up the cereal packs and preserve pots.

'No, thank you. They all stay in the sideboard there. It saves carrying them back and forth. There are boxes for everything in the cupboard.'

Jayne loaded the dishwasher and sat down with a well-earned cup of coffee. Fun? No, it wasn't quite her idea of fun.

'Now, what time do we visit Daniel?' Flora asked, bustling into the kitchen once more.

'After lunch. The children usually visit, too, on a Sunday.

'Shall I start peeling potatoes for lunch?'

Jayne thanked her. At least that might keep Flora busy and out of her way while she cleaned the bedrooms and washed the towels. Thank goodness it was fine today so they could be hung out to dry.

'It's quite hard work running a guest-house, isn't it?' remarked Flora.

Jayne smiled. Flora had no idea just *how* hard.

The days passed fairly quickly for Jayne but she was worried that Flora hadn't been taken out or entertained very well. Eventually, her mother-in-law took it on herself to organise something.

'I was thinking that it might be nice to visit that Eden Project place. I could take the children for the day. How could we get there? Are there buses or trains?'

'I think there are, but I don't know. Perhaps Carl could look it up on the Internet?'

They sorted it all out between themselves and organised a coach trip from a nearby village.

Jayne realised it was bliss to have the place to herself. The party of four had left and only one other couple were staying on. They were no trouble and seemed to come and go happily. Jayne even found an hour or two to do some tidying in the garden. One of Dan's old colleagues was visiting him that afternoon, so she even had that time free. And Chloe was out with Mike, or so she assumed.

⋆ ⋆ ⋆

By the time Jayne finished gardening and went back into the house it was late in the afternoon.

She saw the answering machine light flashing and was annoyed with herself that she hadn't taken the handset out with her. Someone might have been trying to book a room and she could have missed them.

It was a message from Flora, however. Somehow, they'd managed to miss the coach back and there was no other way for them to get home. Would she mind just popping out to fetch them?

It's the best part of an hour each way! Jayne thought angrily. Some '*pop*'. Why couldn't her mother-in-law do even the smallest thing without causing chaos?

Jayne just had to hope the guests didn't get back before she did. She had no idea how she would ever find the family in the huge place that housed the Eden Project. She wondered if one of the children had taken one of their mobile phones and went back to look at the machine. The last number had been dialled from Sarah's mobile. Relieved, she called back and arranged a place to meet.

'Granny's really tired. She wants to sit in the café till you get here,' Sarah said.

'I won't be there for at least an hour, so get her near the gate by then. I don't want to spend ages looking for you and I don't want to have to pay to get in. I'll phone you again when I'm there.'

Angrily she drove away from the house and headed for St Austell. The evening traffic was building up and the roads were busy. It took well over an hour to reach the site, by which time most other people were driving out at the end of the day. At least it meant that she was able to park near the entrance. She pulled out her mobile phone and called Sarah.

'Hi, Mum. Where are you?'

'Walk up the exit path and I'll be waiting for you near the top. Everything OK?'

'Sort of. Granny's very tired and she says her legs hurt. But I think she'll make it.'

'Is she all right?' Jayne asked in some alarm.

'Well, she turned down my offer to go borrow a wheelchair.'

'Good heavens. Do you need me to come down and help?'

'We're on our way. See you in a minute.'

Jayne switched off the phone and gave a sigh. All she needed now was for Flora to need looking after, as well as everything else.

At last, she could see the trio walking slowly up the long path. Carl and Sarah had their gran between them, clearly supporting her as she struggled up the slope.

Jayne hurried forward to assist.

'Oh, thank you, Jayne,' Flora gasped. 'I seem to have worn myself out completely. I couldn't manage to get up to the bus stop in time, but I knew you wouldn't mind fetching us.'

'We must hurry back now.' Jayne was flustered. 'It's very busy on the roads, and if the guests come back they can't get in. I had to leave the house locked up because there was no-one I could ask to stay in. Chloe's off out somewhere.' Jayne hustled them all back to the car and got them settled.

'I hope you had a nice day?'

'Yes, thanks,' the two children replied, in rather flat voices. Jayne caught sight of their faces in the driving mirror. Clearly the day hadn't been quite the success they'd hoped.

'Did you get a meal at lunch-time or just a snack?'

'We had a sandwich,' Flora replied. 'It was all rather expensive, and we knew you'd have a meal ready for us this evening.'

'Well, I haven't started anything yet. I'm here fetching you instead. Maybe we can call for fish and chips on the way back.'

'Oh, I'm not sure my stomach could cope with anything fatty. I'm a martyr to my indigestion, you know.' Flora sounded petulant.

'I hadn't realised — and I've been giving you cooked breakfasts every day. You should have said. Well, it'll have to be something from the freezer, I suppose. It'll take a while before it's ready, of course.'

The traffic was even heavier on the way back, and Jayne felt cross and weary. It took well over an hour to get home, and she still had to start cooking.

'I'd help if I could, dear, but I'm afraid I just can't stand up a moment longer. My ankles are really swollen and my knees ache terribly. I'll go and lie on the sofa and put my feet up for half an hour, if it's all right with you.'

'Fine,' Jayne said resignedly as the phone rang.

It was another guest-house in the village, asking if she could accommodate a family of four who were desperate for somewhere to stay.

'Of course,' she agreed, and wrote down details of their requirements. 'Thanks for passing them on. I'll need half an hour to prepare the rooms.'

'When's supper?' Sarah asked as she came into the kitchen. 'Gran's asking.'

'I've no idea. We've got a family arriving in half an hour and I need to make up two of the beds. Grab some pizzas out of the freezer and put them in the oven, will you? I haven't time to do anything else. I'll make a salad to go with them.'

'And chips?'

'If you like. Your gran won't, but it's too bad.'

Jayne rushed upstairs and grabbed sheets from the airing cupboard to make up two single beds. She put fresh towels in the bathrooms and checked on the double room. It all looked pristine and welcoming.

The doorbell rang and she went down to welcome her guests. Once they were settled in and had been given instructions about finding an evening meal, she was free to return to her own family and the kitchen. She heard raised voices as she opened the door.

'Why on earth are you using frozen chips? We really don't need chips with all that stodge. Tell them, dear,' Flora said, turning to Jayne. 'The silly girl's put a whole tray of chips in the oven as well as the pizza.'

'It's OK, Gran. We always have chips with pizza. And salad. I'm starving so I can easily eat your share.'

'You'll be obese like all the rest of your generation.'

'Please, Flora, don't criticise. This is an emergency, remember. If I hadn't had to drive for over two hours to fetch you back, I would have made a home-cooked meal that even you would have approved of.'

'Really,' her mother-in-law snorted. 'There's no need to be rude. I've struggled into the kitchen to see what I could do to help, and found these poor children trying to cook a meal while you're away doing whatever it is you were doing.'

'I'm trying to earn us some money,' Jayne snapped. 'Now, if you want to help, perhaps you would set the table.'

Angrily Jayne began to wash lettuce and slice tomatoes and cucumber.

When the meal was finally ready, they sat down to eat.

Next second, the door flew open and Mike and Chloe breezed in.

'Just in time, I see. Great — pizza!' Chloe declared. 'Come on, Mike. Grab yourself a plate. Carl, move along and make room for us.'

'I wasn't expecting you both,' Jayne said weakly. 'There isn't enough. Maybe you could put another pizza in the oven? It won't take long.'

'Haven't got time — we're off to a life-saving demo in a few minutes,' said Chloe. 'This is just a refuelling stop.'

'Sorry, Jayne,' Mike apologised. 'Chloe

said it would be all right.'

'Not to worry,' said Jayne. 'It's just been a trying day.'

She felt very close to tears. She was tired and cross and sick of everyone assuming she was there for everything they needed. And Chloe *must* be told that she couldn't keep bringing Mike in for meals.

* * *

It was nine o'clock by the time Jayne was able to sit down. There was a programme on TV that she'd been hoping to watch, but Flora was deeply engrossed in an old film.

Jayne slumped down in an armchair and resigned herself to watching the end of it, which she'd seen several times already.

She began to drift off, and jumped when Flora suddenly spoke.

'Are we having some cocoa tonight, dear?'

'Are you ready for it now?' Jayne

murmured, coming out of her doze.

'Please. I feel very tired tonight. It must be due to all the walking today. I'm not used to it, and public transport is so very tiring.'

'Not that you experienced much of it,' Jayne burst out before she could stop herself.

'What do you mean by that? I only took the children out to give you a break. I thought you'd appreciate some time to relax.'

'It was a nice thought, but I could hardly relax. There was so much to do. Now, have you decided when you're leaving us?'

Flora glared and pursed her mouth.

'I see. You want me to go. I was hoping to spend some time with Daniel when he next comes home. I really don't like hospitals — unhealthy places.'

'Full of sick people,' Jayne said, unable to resist the sarcasm. 'Dan won't be out until at least next weekend and even that's not definite.'

'Well, I've no other plans, and it's so

nice to be able to catch up with Chloe.'

'You've hardly seen her.'

'Well, staying on here would give me a bit more time. I take it she's still welcome here? Or is she to come home with me, too?'

Jayne sighed and wondered how on earth she was supposed to answer that one. Flora was a difficult woman and needed rather more time spent on her than Jayne could spare. She felt mean having such uncharitable thoughts, but really, she'd had enough. Then she had an idea.

'Well, actually, Flora, I've got a number of bookings for next week and need to use your room. If you do want to stay on, I'll have to cancel one pair of guests. I hadn't realised you had so much time free when I accepted the booking.'

Jayne had her fingers crossed behind her back as she told the enormous fib.

Flora looked pained. 'Well, I don't want to be a burden or an inconvenience. I expect you need every penny to pay for this large house. Could you look up train times for me? I expect your so-called guests are wanting the room for the weekend?'

Jayne was saved from further comment by the return of her current family of guests. She went to welcome them in, and to lock the doors.

'What time would you like breakfast?' she asked them, before going to make cocoa for Flora.

★ ★ ★

Things were a little tense next morning, as Flora told her grandchildren that she would be leaving soon. They both smiled, quite unconcerned, which seemed to irritate Flora further.

'I would have stayed longer, but your mother needs my room for paying guests.'

There was still no comment from the children, and Jayne smiled inwardly. They were as wearied by the visit as she was.

'I expect your aunt will be leaving soon as well. She won't want to outstay her welcome either.'

'Oh, I don't think so. She's happy here. She's great fun.'

'But surely you'll need her to move out? I expect her room will be needed, too.'

'No, she's in what's going to be our messing-about room and we don't really need it yet. Besides, she helps Mum all the time.'

'I can't say I've noticed it. She seems to be out most of the time with that boyfriend of hers.'

'I'd better go through to the dining-room and check that the guests have all they need,' said Jayne, deciding it would be diplomatic to get out of Flora's way.

'The guests have gone,' Sarah told her. 'I saw them carrying their luggage out when I came down.'

Jayne gaped at her. 'What? But they can't have gone! They haven't paid! Three rooms, and a huge breakfast, and they've left without paying? I don't believe it — they seemed so nice.'

'Didn't you get their address?' Flora asked.

'Well, yes. They wrote it in the guest book, but if they never intended paying it's unlikely that it was their real address. I'll have to take money in advance in future — it always seems so awful to do that though.'

'And get them to write down their car registration numbers,' Carl suggested. 'I can always go out and check to see if it's the right one.'

'I wonder if Mrs Potts knows anything about them? She sent them to us. I'll give her a call.'

It was all futile. The family had come and gone without any real record being left. Nobody was even certain they'd given their true names.

Carl went into his father's study and turned on the computer.

'Dad's got a programme for finding addresses for his business. I'll try the name and see if it turns up anything. They came from Essex, didn't they?'

'So they said. You'd think they would at least be honest, wouldn't you?'

'Maybe that's how they could afford such a huge car.'

Jayne was still upset. 'You do your best for people and they do this to you. I'll have to get a credit card system set up. Then at least I can take an imprint of the card, like the hotels do. Why are there always so many things to think about?'

When Jayne went back to the kitchen, Flora was washing up at the sink and Sarah was holding a tea towel, protesting that they had a dishwasher for this job.

'It's not worth putting it on for this little bit. Don't complain, dear, and do try to help your mother more — she's obviously finding it very difficult to cope with everything.'

'Thanks, Flora,' said Jayne, as she walked into the room. 'It's very kind of you, but Sarah's right. We do usually use the dishwasher because everything gets sterilised that way. And there are still a lot of dishes left in the dining-room. I'll bring them through.'

Jayne knew that she'd need to put the dishes in the dishwasher later anyway — Flora's eyesight wasn't the best, and her washing up left something to be desired. She would have to wait till she was out of the way, however, or it would lead to further conflict.

Chloe came downstairs as Jayne was going into the dining-room.

''Morning,' she said with a yawn. 'Any coffee going?'

'You'll have to help yourself. But be warned, your mum's in the kitchen. She's taken over the sink and is insisting on washing up.'

'Good old Mum. Trust her not to take the easy way out and use the machine. Hey, what's up, Jayne? You look really upset.'

'I've had some guests check out without paying. Four of them. I'm so angry. And your mother's driving me mad, frankly.'

'And me? What about me? I have a

feeling that I've also done something to incur your displeasure.'

'I've told you before, Chloe — bringing Mike home to meals all the time just isn't on. We don't have the money! And you seem to spend all your time on the beach these days. I'm really grateful for everything you've done to help so far, but I could do with you around a bit more often than you have been lately. Take yesterday — I was completely stuck when I had to fetch the kids and Flora back from the Eden Project. I had to leave the house locked up and the guests couldn't get in.'

'Sorry. But with Mum here, I've been trying to keep out of her way. She keeps asking me to go back with her and start earning a living,' Chloe explained dolefully. 'But you're right. I'm not making any contribution to this place. I bring Mike back because it's my way of thanking him for treating me to meals and drinks. I've got no money left. I didn't have much when I came back, but it's all gone now. I'll have to get a job and stop messing around. Leave it to me. I'll make it up to you. I'll start by cleaning the rooms. You go and do some gardening, or something that you enjoy.'

Chloe gave her a hug, and Jayne immediately felt tears of self-pity burning her eyes. She hadn't realised just how stressed she had become.

'Thanks, Chloe. That's good of you. And I think I've upset your mother, too. I lied to her. I told her that her room is booked for the weekend, so that she would go.'

Chloe roared with laughter.

'Well, we'll just have to keep up the pretence, won't we? I'll take her to see Dan this afternoon and try to organise her departure — get tickets and so on.'

'Thanks. I hope you can do it without mortally offending her. The thought of having her around for another week or even two . . . I'm sorry, I shouldn't speak about your mother like this.'

'It's all right. I've known her a lot

longer than you have. Why do you think I went abroad for so long? And why do you think I'm here and not at home with her? I do love her, but she's so difficult to live with. I just can't keep up with her standards.'

'Thanks, Chloe. And I'm sorry I moaned about you bringing Mike home. I'd never have coped with all this without your help — or his.'

* ⋆ ⋆ ⋆ *

Chloe went missing for much of the morning, but returned at lunchtime ready to drive her mother to the hospital. She looked pleased with herself, but would say nothing about where she had been.

Jayne brought in the washing and put it away in the airing cupboard. She'd already cleaned the guest-rooms and made some of the beds, ready for anyone else who turned up. It was the end of half-term week, so she didn't really expect anyone, but in the world of the seaside landlady one simply never knew.

Then, as it was potentially Flora's last evening, Jayne decided to make a special supper and put a roast into the oven and made an apple pie.

It was sunny and quite warm outside and so, chores done, she wandered out into the garden. There was still so much to be done out there. She should put in some summer bedding plants to cheer up the borders near the house, at least — but it would be expensive and it would mean even more digging. Eventually, she would plant the borders with herbaceous plants that would flower year after year and give minimal work. Surely things would get easier as time went on? She wouldn't have to cope with Dan in hospital forever, and if he could build up his clients, they would be better off financially.

But Jayne was beginning to wonder if her husband would ever be quite the same again — if he would ever be able to walk properly unaided.

Despite everything, though, she felt a grain of pride in all she had achieved.

She saw the car coming up the hill and went back into the house to put the kettle on.

'How was he?' she asked brightly when Flora and Chloe came in.

'Still quite poorly, I'm afraid,' Flora reported.

Jayne raised her eyebrows questioningly to Chloe, who shook her head in denial.

'He's so worried about you, dear. He thinks — well, we all think you're working too hard. I told him about those people absconding this morning. He's very concerned about the safety of his family, having people like that in the house.'

Jayne sighed. 'You shouldn't have worried him. I wasn't going to tell him about it.'

'And he was most upset that I'm going to leave. I won't see him again for months probably. Still, I explained about you needing my room and he sort of understood. He did suggest that I might stay somewhere else and be able to visit him. But I said I couldn't possibly expect him to pay for me to stay somewhere else.'

'Would you like some tea, Mum?' Chloe interrupted. 'I see Jayne's boiled the kettle. Perhaps you'd like to go into the lounge and I'll bring it through for you?'

'I could certainly do with a cup,' complained Flora. 'It's so unbearably hot in that hospital — I feel quite dehydrated.'

'Is he really so poorly?' Jayne asked Chloe anxiously when Flora finally left the room.

'Of course not. He's fine. But you know how Mother likes to dramatise everything. She's feeling sorry for herself. And don't worry, Dan never once suggested paying for her to stay somewhere else. That was just her little fantasy. We called at the station on the way back and got her ticket for eleven o'clock tomorrow morning.'

'Thanks so much, Chloe. You're a star.'

'But you'll have to take her to the station, I'm afraid. I'll be working,' Chloe announced, a touch of pride in her voice.

'What do you mean?'

'I got myself a job today. I start tomorrow at seven, so I hope someone's got an alarm clock I can borrow! Don't look like that. It's only in the village shop, but at least there will be some money at the end of the week.'

They all spent a happy evening together; even Carl and Sarah enjoyed themselves. They played several games of Scrabble and giggled over some of the silly words that Chloe suggested. Flora approved of the meal and even accepted a glass of wine. Everyone seemed to be relieved that the week was over. The children still had a couple of days before they went back to school, so they were still enjoying their freedom.

As Flora went up to bed, she promised she would vacate her room before breakfast, in case the new guests arrived early. The children gave their mother a startled look and she smiled sweetly at them, and thanked her mother-in-law profusely for her thoughtfulness.

Chloe was busying herself packing away the Scrabble board to cover her own sniggers. 'I'll go and make cocoa shall I?' she offered.

★　★　★

The house seemed peaceful, if not rather empty, after Flora's departure. Jayne felt guilty as there were no guests booked in at all. She'd hoped she might get some passing tourists who'd travelled down without booking accommodation in advance, but this was not to be.

At around five o'clock, Chloe came home looking worn out.

'I've been busy all day, but very bored, at the checkout. My neck aches like crazy after picking stuff up and scanning it all day. And people are so rude at times. The wages aren't much, but it's really only temporary.'

'Are you staying in this evening or are you going to be out?' Jane asked her.

'I'm supposed to be going out for drinks with the surfers but I'm almost too tired, although I expect once I've had a shower and something to eat I'll feel better. Meantime, I could murder a cuppa. Is Dan OK? And did you get Mum on to the train?'

'Yes and yes. And the kettle's boiled. And no guests. I feel dreadful about shooing your mother away like that.'

'I don't. It's a great relief.'

'You're dreadful, Chloe.' But Jayne couldn't help grinning. 'Almost as bad as me.'

Chloe On The Run!

The following week was much less tense. Even though Jayne was working as hard as ever, driving back and forth to the hospital and endlessly making beds, cleaning, and washing, she felt more relaxed.

There were times when she still wondered if she was doing the right thing — it was such very hard work — and she wondered, briefly, if she could afford to take on someone to help with the cleaning, but the business was still too precarious to make such a decision.

All week, there had been a steady trickle of visitors, but none of them stayed for more than a night or two. She'd offered a discount for a stay of more than three nights, hoping to get week-long bookings, but most people wanted to tour around and were happy to book a place for a short stay, then move on.

What she needed now was to get some firm bookings for the summer holidays, and she splashed out on an advert in a holiday magazine that sold nationally. It was very expensive, but she and Dan had talked it through and decided it was worth the outlay. If they weren't full for the summer, they would have nothing to fall back on during the winter months.

Dan, still stuck in what he called his *dratted wheelchair*, was starting to feel less optimistic about his own earning potential.

★   ★   ★

Jayne was driving back from the hospital one afternoon when her mobile rang. She pulled over to answer it and listened in horror as the children's headmaster spoke. Would she please come to the school as soon as possible, as there had been an incident and he

245

felt it best if Carl was removed from the premises.

'But what's he done?' she demanded.

'I'll explain when you get here. Can you come right away, please?'

'I'll be there as soon as I can.'

She worried all the way. What did he mean by 'an incident'? And why should Carl need to be removed from the premises? It all sounded most alarming and very unlike her son. He was usually well behaved and hated fighting or arguments of any sort. Jayne pulled up outside the school and took a deep breath to steady her nerves. She hurried inside and looked around for the correct door. Seeing the headmaster's name, she knocked on the glass panel.

'Ah, Mrs Pearson? I'm sorry to bother you but there's been a spot of bother.'

'Carl is all right, isn't he? Is he hurt in some way?'

'He's fine. But he was fighting with one of the other boys at lunchtime.'

'That's most unlike Carl.'

'It wasn't all his fault. But then it never is, is it? He was defending his sister, from what I can gather. Typical playground battles — name-calling and so on.'

'So what exactly happened?'

'Carl punched another boy and a brawl started, with several children becoming involved. I separated them, and the other parents are on their way to pick up their children. Now, I know there have been problems for you, but I think I have to insist that Carl stays home for the rest of this week. I'll send work for him and then I shall expect an apology on Monday, first thing, when he returns. I'm sure I can rely on you, Mrs Pearson, to supervise him and ensure that the work is completed.'

'Of course. But whatever you say, I shall be anxious to hear his side of it all and then I shall punish him myself as I see fit.'

'Fair enough. I know I can rely on you to do the right thing. I'll ask my secretary to collect him, and perhaps

Sarah could bring his work home for him?'

Jayne nodded, feeling sick. How could her son have done something so terrible that he needed three days to cool off?

Carl had a bloody nose and looked very white when he arrived at the headmaster's study.

'I'm sorry, sir,' he volunteered. 'I didn't mean to cause any trouble.'

'Your mother will take you home now, and she knows what needs to be done. I shall see you on Monday morning at eight-thirty sharp.'

Jayne and Carl walked out to the car in silence. Jayne couldn't trust herself to speak just yet. She felt hurt, betrayed, and angry, but she wanted to hear Carl's version of events before she vented her feelings.

One of the school buses was turning into the drive.

'I'll pull to one side and wait for Sarah.'

They sat quietly, neither willing to

broach the subject of his apparent disgrace. A steady stream of children poured out of the building and several stared into the car, some making faces. Carl sank back in his seat as if trying to disappear into it. At last Sarah appeared and began to trudge down the long drive. Jayne lowered the window and called to her. Sarah turned and climbed into the car.

'I gather you've heard?' she said.

'Some of it. I'll hear the rest when we get home.'

The drive home was conducted in total silence, so different from their usual chatter.

Jayne led the way into the house, and glanced at the phone. The light was flashing with messages. The first was the headmaster, repeating his request for her to come to school, and the second was someone who left a mobile number, looking for accommodation. The next message was an almost familiar gruff voice telling Chloe that if she didn't return the call, she and her family would be sorry.

'What next?' Jayne muttered as she called back the would-be guests.

They were a couple wanting a room for two nights, so she agreed to put them up.

Her own family drama would have to fit in around them.

Jayne and the children ate a subdued meal and gradually the story came out. Several of the boys had been calling Sarah names and teasing her because she'd fallen behind with some work. She'd also dared to say that she didn't like some boy band or other that was rated very highly by everyone else. When the boys had started pulling Sarah's bag to pieces, Carl had jumped in and punched them. Being a strong boy, he'd managed to inflict several black eyes and start a couple of nose-bleeds.

'It's so unfair, Mum. I was only trying to stop them from hurting Sarah.'

'Maybe you were. But you need to

learn to control your temper and not use violence to sort out these problems. You've never done anything like it before.'

'I've never had to,' he said reasonably.

'Well, you've only been suspended for a few days. You can do your work at home and apologise, and that will be the end of it — I hope.'

'OK, Mum,' he mumbled. 'I'm sorry.'

'Where's Chloe?' asked Sarah. 'She's usually home by now.'

'Ah, yes. Chloe,' Jayne said, remembering the threatening phone call. 'I'm not sure where she is. She must have gone straight out with Mike. Now, clear this lot away, will you? Load it into the machine. I must go and check that everything's ready for the guests.'

* * *

Carl had completed all his homework by soon after lunch the next day.

'It's actually OK working at home,' he told his mum. 'What should I do now?'

'How about reading some of your set books? Get ahead a little. It would be nice if you could get yourself back to the top of the class.'

'I guess so. I have been getting behind with school a bit. I don't think I realised just how much I miss Dad — and I'm worried about him too.

'I will try to get on better at school, though. I promise. I'm sorry to have given you so much hassle.'

His voice broke a little as he spoke, and he didn't object when Jayne gave him a hug.

'Oh, love, I'm sorry too. I've been neglecting you, but it's been such hard work to get this place straight and to try to keep Dad's spirits up too. Things must start to get better soon — they must!'

When Chloe arrived home that evening with Mike in tow, she looked very pleased with herself.

'I come bearing gifts,' she yelled from the door. 'Come on in, Mike.'

Jayne was in the kitchen making new

batches of scones for the visitors.

'Here you are — with my love.'

She dumped several large trays of bedding plants on the kitchen table.

'We had them left over when we closed today, and the shop decided we might never sell them, so I did a deal. There are five more trays outside. Mike drove me home with them.'

'That's very kind but where on earth am I going to put them? And take them away from my baking, please. They're dripping soil and water everywhere.'

Jayne felt like weeping. Normally she would have been delighted with such a gift. The plants would be lovely to have, but she'd need to dig the borders over to plant them, and she didn't have time.

'Sorry, Chloe, it's a lovely thought and something I'd have loved to buy myself, when the time was right.'

'I didn't think,' Chloe replied in a small voice. 'Maybe they'll be OK just left in the trays for a few days?'

'Maybe. Perhaps Carl could do some digging as a punishment,' she muttered.

'Are you here for supper, Mike?'

'Well, if you're sure,' he began. 'But I'm really here because I wanted to talk to you. About the outbuilding project?'

'I'm sorry, but there *is* no project,' Jayne said slightly snappily.

'Just plans, then. As I said, I need to do some stuff for my course. I wanted to take some photographs — I hoped you wouldn't mind.'

'No, of course not,' Jayne said with a sigh. 'Mike, I don't mind you taking photographs or doing anything else that will help you with your college course. But, however good your plans are, we haven't the money to go ahead with them.'

'Fine. But just assuming there was money, what exactly would Dan need for his office space? Have you any idea what sort of lay-out he'd want?'

'I don't know. Maybe a small reception area, with somewhere for his secretary to work, and a space for clients to sit while waiting — and a cloakroom.'

'And suppose he still needed to use a wheelchair to get around? He'd need wider doorways and an accessible cloakroom. Lower desks and door handles. Even remote-controlled door openings,' suggested Mike.

'Oh, heavens, I hadn't thought about that,' said Jayne.

'I'll go and take some pictures now, if that's all right?'

Jayne was thoughtful. If Dan needed to use the wheelchair long-term, there were going to be problems with access everywhere in the house.

Chloe was setting the table when the phone rang.

'Get that, would you, Chloe? I'm dishing up.'

'Hello?' Chloe said as she picked up the phone. 'Sea Haven — accommodation available.'

Suddenly her tone changed completely.

'What? Oh, it's you. No. I'm not interested. Go away and stop bothering me. No. Leave us alone. I don't want to know.' She was almost shouting into the phone.

'Chloe, love, what is it?' whispered Jayne. Chloe waved her away.

'No, *you* listen! If you even think of touching any one of my family, you'll be very sorry indeed. No, I will not.' Chloe slammed the phone down and rushed away to her bedroom, slamming the door behind her.

Jayne followed her and knocked on her door

'Chloe, what was all that about?' she called out. The one-sided conversation that Jayne had overheard was clearly some sort of threat to her sister-in-law, and possibly to the whole family.

'Nothing to concern you. I'm dealing with it,' Chloe shouted back through the closed door. 'I'll be down for supper in a minute.'

Jayne heard sounds of banging and crashes — what on earth was Chloe doing?

Eventually, after waiting for Chloe on the landing for several minutes, Jayne went back downstairs to the kitchen.

Mike came in from the outbuildings, looking very pleased with himself.

'I've got some great shots and some great ideas. It's a potential gold mine out there. You might even get a grant to cover some of the development. It would be worth asking. Where's Chloe?'

'She's coming — she's up in her room. Someone phoned her and upset her, but she won't say anything about it. I'll just call the kids and we can eat.'

They didn't wait for Chloe, and she still hadn't appeared by the time they'd finished pudding.

'Just go up and see what she's doing, will you?' Jayne asked Sarah.

Sarah came back after a few minutes.

'Mum, I think she's left! Her back-pack's missing and she's nowhere around. Most of her clothes seem to have gone, too.'

'How can she have gone?' Mike demanded. 'She doesn't have a car. And anyway, why would she just go off without saying anything?'

'Dad always said that was the kind of thing she did,' Sarah put in, looking lost and afraid.

'I'll go and look for her,' Mike said urgently. 'She can't have got far at this time of day. Where might she be headed?'

'I've no idea,' Jayne said.

'Do you know who it was who phoned and upset her?'

'Try dialling one-four-seven-one,' suggested Carl.

Mike did so. 'I think that's a London code. Maybe she's gone to the station. I'll try there first. Thanks for supper, Jayne. I'll call you later.' He rushed out and she heard his tyres screech as he drove away far too fast.

Jayne went back inside. She was terribly worried. The caller must have been the same one that had called earlier and he didn't sound a nice man at all.

What on earth had Chloe done to know such a person? Surely she couldn't be involved in anything criminal? Not Chloe. She was always so honest. But then, she had been very cagey about her sudden departure from Malaysia.

'Do you want to play cards or a board game or something?' Jayne suggested to the children, but they didn't answer.

'Why do you think Chloe's disappeared so suddenly?' Sarah asked.

'I really don't know. Shall we watch something? Video or DVD — or maybe there's something on television you'd like to watch?'

'I might read,' Carl said miserably.

★ ★ ★

It was after nine before Mike phoned. He'd been to every railway station in the area but none of them had seen Chloe or anyone fitting her description. He'd also been to all the bus stations, and finally driven some miles along the main road in case she was trying to hitch a lift.

'I'll phone Flora tomorrow, in case

she turns up there. But thanks, Mike. Thanks very much. Keep in touch, won't you?' Jayne told him.

Once the guests were in, Jayne locked the doors and they all went to bed, but she slept badly, anxious about her sister-in-law. They had become close over the past weeks and she was disappointed that there was something going on in Chloe's life that she hadn't felt able to share.

Jayne got up early, prepared the breakfast, and wished away the time till she could phone Flora. She finally called at nine-thirty.

'Flora? It's Jayne. How are you?'

'I'm sure you're not really interested, Jayne. Why are you phoning? Is there something wrong with Daniel?'

'No, he's fine. Progressing as much as one could hope for. No, it's Chloe. She left us last night and I wondered if she had arrived home. To you, I mean?'

'She'd hardly do that, would she? Now, if you'll excuse me, I have a lot to do.'

The phone slammed down at the other end of the line, and Jayne felt tears burning once more. She felt very guilty about sending Flora home.

She sighed and began stacking the dishwasher once more. Life seemed one long round of dirty dishes and soggy towels, not to mention all the other troubles that had landed on them.

The weekend was long and empty. The usual succession of hospital visits and visitors came and went and Carl returned to school on Monday armed with a perfectly-written apology, all his own work, and a very contrite attitude.

Nobody had heard a word from Chloe and even Mike had been absent from their lives.

It was a week later before, at long last, they had news of Chloe.

Jayne was about to leave the house to collect Dan, to bring him home for the weekend, when the phone rang.

'Jayne? It's Chloe. I'm so sorry about leaving you like that.'

'Are you all right? Where are you?'

'I'm in London.'

'But why are you there? Why did you go? Please, come back to us.'

'I can't. But thanks for wanting me to. I just wanted you to know I'm all right. It's all a mess, but honestly, I'm OK. I'm coping with it. I hope everything's going well for you. Give my love to Dan and the kids.'

'But, Chloe, why is this necessary?'

'Lots of love. Bye.'

'But, Chloe . . . ' Jayne's voice trailed off as the line went dead. She dialled one-four-seven-one, but the caller's number had been withheld.

'Oh, Chloe, what have you done?'

She called Mike but only got voicemail. She left him a message asking him to call as soon as possible, and then drove to the hospital to collect Dan.

She told him about Chloe's call as they drove home.

'Sounds like a typical Chloe drama — something and nothing. She's always liked to make her life seem like one drama after another. Don't worry, she'll come back when she's ready. Now, tell me how you've been getting on this week?'

That was one good thing, thought Jayne. At least Dan seemed to be showing an interest in things at last.

* * *

On the whole, Dan's weekend at home was a success. He and Jayne discussed several plans to expand the business, including the possibility of making some alterations to the outbuildings.

Dan seemed excited by Mike's suggestions and ideas, and phoned him to ask if he would call round to the house to talk them over.

'I think we might be able to afford to do it if we work carefully,' Dan told Jayne. 'After all, if I do get the accountancy business going, I'll need a place to work. I can hardly work in my bedroom, can I? Let's just see how it goes. Is that Mike now? I think I can hear a car.'

When Mike came inside, Jayne thought he looked upset. He'd lost his usually sunny demeanour and seemed stressed.

'Look, I'd better tell you right away that I won't be able to do any more work for you. Dad's almost back to normal and I have my own work to get on with,' he said.

'I'm sorry about that,' said Dan. 'We were thinking of going ahead with the office project, keeping the plans pretty much as you suggested.'

'Well, maybe you can get someone else to draw up plans for you,' said Mike.

'What's happened, Mike? There's something wrong, isn't there? Is it to do with Chloe?' Jayne asked him.

Mike shrugged. 'Chloe's back in her old life in London. She won't let me near her. So, that's that.'

He looked thoroughly miserable and bewildered at the way things had turned out.

'I thought I'd found the one, you

know? We got on so well and she seemed to return my feelings, but now it's ice-maiden time and I'm being frozen out, so it seems.'

'So, you *have* been in touch?'

'I went to see her in London — tracked her down. I spent hours looking for her in all her old haunts. She'd told me places she used to go and mentioned a few names. It took time, but finally I found her. She's working in a shop and staying with a friend. Sleeping on the floor and looking dreadful. She's lost weight, even in a couple of weeks, and all her sparkle's gone.'

'But you must know what's happened? Is she in some sort of trouble?'

'You could say that.'

'Come on, Mike. Tell us the whole story.'

'She swore me to secrecy.' Mike paused and looked at their anxious faces. 'Oh, all right. But she'll be furious with me for worrying you.'

'We're already worried half to death

— she's our family!'

Mike began his tale.

'Did she ever talk to you about a guy called Alistair?'

Jayne nodded.

'The ex,' said Mike. 'Well, it seems he was involved in some shady deals in Malaysia . . . some sort of fraud. Chloe and Alistair were working for a charity and he was pocketing the funds. The charity found out and are taking action against him. Chloe was horrified when she found out what he'd been up to, and finished with him.

'He'd asked her to marry him, bought her a ring and everything — though he'd even bought that in some dodgy deal, using charity funds.

'She gave in her notice to the charity and came back here. Now Alistair has followed her, and he says he'll drag her into the scandal if she doesn't go back to him. When I turned up he threatened me, too, and said he'd sling mud at Chloe's entire family.

'She knows you two have had enough

bad luck for one year and wants to spare you any embarrassment or more hassle. It seems that Alistair knows a whole lot of undesirable characters and has any number of scams going on.'

'What on earth did she ever see in the man?'

'He's a very plausible liar — has a great deal of charm, apparently, though I didn't see it when I met him. I called the police and Chloe went nuts and sent me packing. I just had to give up and come back here. She wouldn't let me help her, and she wanted you kept out of it all.'

'What a mess! Poor Chloe — what a waster he turned out to be!' Dan commented. 'And to think she's thrown you over because of him . . . '

Mike stood up abruptly. 'Maybe Dad will be able to offer some help with building work in a few weeks, if you're still interested. By the way, I meant to ask before — I assume you got planning permission for change of use before you started your B and B business?'

'I didn't think we had to. It was a hotel once. Then a nursing home.'

'Well,' said Mike, shrugging, 'it might be worth checking before someone comes to inspect you.'

'Oh no! I don't believe it. Is there anything else that can go wrong? That's all we need.' Dan put his head in his hands.

'Can you give us a contact number for Chloe?' Jayne asked. 'We really must talk to her. We might be able to persuade her to return.'

'I doubt you will if I couldn't. She'll be furious with me for telling you anything, and even more so if I give you the number, but please call her. I don't want to lose her.'

He scribbled down the number and gave it to Jayne.

Come Home, Chloe!

Jayne called the number that Mike had given her, but it took several attempts before she got an answer. The girl who answered was reluctant to call Chloe to the phone but, eventually, after much whispering in the background, Chloe spoke.

'Jayne, I'm sorry to do this to you. How did you get my number? Of course — Mike.'

'I forced it out of him. Please come back, Chloe. I'm sure we can help you. We miss you. There's nothing this ex of yours can do to harm you.'

'You don't understand. He knows a lot of dangerous men. I was completely taken in by him. I don't even know why he was in Malaysia to start with. He's not interested in helping anyone but himself. He's charming and attractive — and thoroughly nasty. If I don't go back to him he's going to drag my name through the mud along with his.'

'Then you have to come back to safety. How can you even consider going back to him? He only wants to use you.'

'I know. I feel so stupid. But if I'm near him in London, at least you'll all be out of harm's way.'

'Come back, Chloe,' Jayne pleaded. 'We want you here with us.'

There was the sound of quiet sobbing and then silence.

'Please, Chloe,' Jayne repeated, clutching the receiver so tightly that her hand ached.

Several minutes went by, with no answer from Chloe.

'All right then,' Chloe whispered at last. 'Thanks for not hating me. I can't wait to see you all again — and Sea Haven.'

'And Mike?'

'I doubt if he'll ever speak to me again. I'll be back very soon, I promise.'

★   ★   ★

It was Monday morning before Chloe finally arrived, looking scruffy and exhausted.

She had hitched down again, despite everyone's dire warnings, arriving somewhere near the Devon border at dawn, and catching a bus for the last leg of her journey.

'I need coffee and a shower and then I'll start to function again,' she told them.

Dan was due back in hospital in an hour, but he insisted on hearing the whole story before he and Jayne left. There was little to add to what Chloe had already told them, so Jayne and Dan spent the time persuading her never to dash away like that again.

'And when you've had your shower and some food, you must phone Mike. He's been wonderful — and I know he cares for you,' Jayne told her.

'Thanks so much for your concern.' She gave them both hugs and went upstairs to settle back in.

Jayne turned to Dan.

'We'd better get you back to hospital, I suppose,' she said sadly. 'It'll be great when all this is over and you're back home again permanently.'

'Tell me about it. I hate leaving you all — especially now.'

When she returned from the hospital, Mike's car was parked outside and Jayne smiled to see it. Inside, Mike and Chloe were sitting in the warm kitchen, holding hands and looking very contented.

'He's forgiven me,' Chloe said happily. 'We're going to check out the surf later. Can we have something to eat first? Is there anything in the fridge?'

'You could always have a breakfast. I do a good full English, hadn't you heard?'

'Oh, Jayne! One of your breakfasts would be absolute heaven.'

Then the phone rang with a booking and Jayne's life began to get back to what had become normal.

★   ★   ★

The weather was hot and sunny, and in Cornwall the summer season was in full swing. Holidaymakers poured into the county, all of them needing accommodation.

Jayne was rushed off her feet, and Chloe became the chief chambermaid each morning.

She wasn't the most efficient worker, prone to stopping to gaze out of the window, or to dash off to test the surf when the mood took her — but Jayne was grateful for any help at all.

Several times people turned up at the door wanting a room and Jayne had to turn them away.

'It's a pity we didn't finish the rest of the house,' Jayne muttered about twice a day.

The smaller rooms would be really useful, especially for families with older children.

Jane decided that they really would have to get them decorated over the winter. And they would have to make a start on Dan's offices as soon as they could.

'Once Mike's surf competition is over, he'll submit the plans,' said Chloe.

'You're really happy with him, aren't you?' Jayne asked, pulling sheets off a bed.

'Oh, Jayne, he's the most wonderful man I've ever met. How I could ever have fallen for a man like Alistair, I'll never know.'

'I'm really pleased for you,' Jayne told her, struggling with a pile of laundry. 'Now, back to the vacuum cleaner, please — we've got more guests coming in soon.'

Life seemed to be on course again for all of them, thought Jayne happily.

However, as the holiday season was drawing to a close, she began to worry about money. She had saved as much as she could all through the summer, so the next few weeks were taken care of, but bills would keep on coming in throughout the year, and it was something of a concern.

* * *

Then, one day an official-looking letter arrived for Chloe. Jayne watched anxiously as she opened it. Her sister-in-law turned pale and sat down heavily.

'What is it?'

'It's Alistair. He's been arrested and the court case comes up in three weeks. They say I have to go and testify. Oh, Jayne, I'm scared. Who knows what he'll do to stop me?'

'He won't know where to find you.'

'But the police know where I am. They sent this letter, didn't they? What's it going to do to the children and Dan? And your business? We can't have protection twenty-four hours a day and he knows some very dodgy characters. They scared me half to death most of the time.'

When Chloe broke the news to Mike, he insisted that he should move into the house temporarily.

'I can sleep in Dan's room downstairs while he's away and the couch will do me when he's home. That way,

I'll be here to hear if anyone tries to get in.'

'It's very good of you but I can't ask all this of you,' Jayne protested.

'It's my pleasure. It means I can keep a proper eye on this woman of ours,' Mike said, with a tender smile in Chloe's direction. 'And I'll come with you to London, Chloe, when the case comes up. Now stop looking so worried, all of you.'

'I love you, Mike Polglaze,' Chloe burst out, flinging her arms round him.

'I think I do too,' Jayne murmured.

★ ★ ★

The weeks leading up to Alistair's trial were stressful and tempers were often short.

Jayne insisted on taking the children everywhere and picking them up, too, 'just in case', much to their disgust.

Chloe and Mike stayed at the house, keeping a careful watch on anyone who came near as they worked.

They even gave up their beloved surfing for a few weeks and Mike had the brilliant idea of setting up a video recorder and camera so that anyone who came up the drive had their presence recorded.

However, as the day of the hearing in London came close, there was good news about Dan — the news they'd all been waiting for. He was to return home permanently at the end of the week!

★   ★   ★

Everyone was overjoyed to see Dan back. He was still limited in what he could do, and he still needed to use the wheelchair much of the time, but at long last he was home, finally and for good.

Chloe and Mike left for the court appearance, and Jayne and Dan felt more relaxed. If Alistair was sent to prison, some of their worries would be over for a while, at least.

'Will you help me to get upstairs?' Dan asked Jayne. 'I really want to see what you've done up there — I've only seen photographs!'

'Are you sure you can manage it?' Jayne was anxious.

'If you help. I've been practising on stairs at the hospital.'

Slowly, they struggled upstairs together, Dan clinging to the banisters with Jayne on the other side of him.

He was exhausted but triumphant when he reached the top.

She handed him his crutches and he went from room to room, exclaiming with delight.

'It's fantastic! You're a miracle worker — and I just don't know how you've done it all for the price. Did you really get all this furniture at an auction?'

'Of course. Chloe helped too — bidding for the wrong items and then negotiating an excellent price to sell on the rubbish she'd bought.' Jayne laughed at the memory.

Dan grinned. 'Jayne, you've worked

wonders, and now I'm back, I want to do my part in everything. It's been a long hard slog, but I'm BACK!'

'Now all we have to do is get you back downstairs again.'

'That's easy,' he said cheerfully, and somehow managed to hop down using one crutch and the banister rail. 'I'll soon be able to sleep upstairs again. That'll be such a relief.'

Jayne smiled happily.

★   ★   ★

When the full details of Alistair's misdeeds came out, Chloe's part in his life proved to be a very small portion in the grand scheme of things. No one could understand why he'd been so keen to have Chloe back with him, unless it was that he needed to think he could control her in some way. He was given a long sentence, along with several of his so-called friends.

Chloe and Mike came back to Cornwall, greatly relieved. Mike was able to settle back to his final year of study and Chloe found a job in a local children's home.

'I might as well make use of my limited talents,' she said happily. 'After all, if I could cope with a dozen orphans with no facilities or equipment, I can surely be of some use here.'

Jayne decided to bite the bullet with the planning authorities and ask about the planning permission she should have had before she'd opened for business. Mike helped her to fill in the forms, and after several weeks of anxious waiting, the officer called round to inspect the property. He was satisfied that all the safety rules had been covered and supplied the necessary paperwork.

'You should contact your mother, too,' Jayne told Dan. 'I've been feeling awful about her and the way she left — she clearly doesn't want anything to do with me any more.'

'She'll come round. I don't blame you for sending her packing. She always was a difficult lady, and a week of her's enough to drive anyone potty!'

★   ★   ★

As winter began to bite, they listened to the winds howling around the old house and felt safe and warm inside.

'Summer seems a long way off,' said Jayne one evening.

'Maybe we should think of some way to attract custom over the winter,' Dan said thoughtfully. 'Start courses or something. Cookery or writing. Or painting. There are heaps of things we could do.'

'And if we made something of the outbuildings, that would give us accommodation for it. Do we know anyone who could run them?'

They began planning and were excited by all their new ideas.

'This is all very well, but we have to live for the rest of this year and through to next season,' said Dan. 'It's really time I began to organize my accountancy business. Until the new office is built, I'll use the room we'd originally planned to use. Could you bring me the files out of the utility room? It's time I got myself organised.'

Dan worked hard for the next few days, scribbling furiously on endless pieces of paper. He was happy and seemed much more like his old self.

'We need to get the computer set-up changed,' he said. 'I can't manage with it in that corner. Too cramped.'

'You need a proper computer station — they have some on special offer at the big stores,' Chloe told him.

'Can't you find one in an auction sale somewhere?' Dan grinned. 'I'd like to see you in action.'

Within a few weeks, Dan had put some adverts in the local paper offering accountancy services and had received a few enquiries. He hoped to set up a few contacts in time for the end of the tax year rush, knowing from past experience that many people left things to the last minute and then needed someone like himself to help when they found themselves unable to cope. His advert included reference to tax returns and, as he had hoped, a couple of small businesses signed on.

⋆　⋆　⋆

Dan persevered with his exercises and soon found himself growing in both strength and confidence.

Then, one Sunday near Christmas, the family heard him calling urgently from the lounge. They rushed in, dreading something drastic had happened.

Far from it. As they came in, he got up from the sofa where he'd been reading the Sunday papers and, without using his crutches, he walked slowly over to the fireplace. He was slightly unsteady, and sweating with the effort, but he'd done it — he'd walked unaided for the first time.

'I feel like a baby who's just taken his

first steps,' he laughed. 'Now all I have to do is get back to where I was, and sit down again.'

'Well done, Dad,' Sarah said, her eyes shining in delight.

'Yeah, cool!' Carl agreed.

Jayne couldn't quite manage to speak. She was so thrilled, she didn't trust her voice to work properly.

'I'll phone Mum and tell her the good news,' Dan said once he was safely back in his seat.

'Best of luck,' Jayne said wryly

She was still in Flora's bad books, even though Dan had tried to encourage his mother to see what a huge amount of work Jayne had undertaken.

'I thought, perhaps, I should invite her for Christmas?' suggested Dan. 'What do you think? It's only three weeks away — it might cheer her up.'

'Why not? At least if you're here I don't have to do all the entertaining.'

Flora was delighted by the invitation and agreed to come in good time to help Jayne get things ready for the big day.

'Oh, dear, here we go again,' Jayne groaned. 'But maybe if I'm not so stressed with visitors, I'll be able to cope with her better.'

'And we're all here to help — aren't we, kids?' Dan grinned at Jayne and reached for her hand. 'We might even be able to afford a small Christmas present for each of them — a packet of chocolate each and maybe a tangerine in their stockings.'

'Gosh, thanks,' laughed Sarah.

'This place is going to take a lot of decorating,' Carl mused as he looked at the wide staircase and huge hall. 'We'll need at least two trees and loads of lights. We have to make it look really good. We should have a party, too. We can ask everyone who helped us out.'

'Well, I'm not really sure . . . ' Jayne began.

'I think it's a brilliant idea. Well done, Carl,' Dan enthused. 'It's about time we had a major celebration. And you never know, there may be a few clients among the group. Shall we make it a pizza party?'

'No, no, no,' Jayne protested, laughing. 'No more pizzas — please!'

'Well, I think you should let me organise the music,' insisted Carl.

'No,' Sarah objected. 'Tell him, Mum — nobody but him *likes* his music.'

'Gosh, it's good to be back with my family again,' Dan laughed. 'I've really missed the squabbling.'

★　★　★

The party was arranged for the weekend before Christmas, two days before Flora was due to arrive. They had all agreed that she would hate a rowdy party and it would probably put a damper on things if she were there.

All their old friends came, along with several new families from the village whose children had become friends with Carl and Sarah. It was quite a houseful and everyone had brought food and wine to share. It was a lovely atmosphere and the old house rejoiced in having its rooms filled again. They all trooped round looking at the finished rooms and admiring the furnishings.

'It looks wonderful! When you think back to what it was like the weekend of the peeling party,' said Claire's husband, Bill.

'And don't forget the purple woodwork,' Claire added. 'I love the way you've decorated the stairs with evergreen garlands. Very festive.'

'We'll be forever grateful to everyone, the way you all turned out to help us in our hour of need. And we've certainly made a good start with the bed and breakfast this season. Next year will be even better, once we've got a proper website and things are better organised.'

Jayne went on to regale their friends with tales of her failures and the lessons she had learned — the Harrisons, who'd eaten everything in sight, and the family who'd left without paying

— 'But, fortunately, although there might be a few nasty people and the odd crook going around, I think we can honestly say how lucky we are that most folk we know are lovely!'

It was a jolly evening and they finally sank into bed in the early hours, happy and satisfied that the year was ending so well.

'Only four days till Christmas,' Jayne said sleepily.

Christmas at Sea Haven

Any misgivings over Flora's visit were quickly dispelled. Jayne greeted her at the station and took her suitcase as if nothing had ever been amiss. So long as Flora didn't mention her hurried departure at the end of her last visit, neither would Jayne.

'Good trip?' Jayne asked her, waiting for the usual saga of what had gone wrong and who had failed to give up their seat for her. But it never came.

'Not bad at all. Such a nice young man helped me with my luggage and chatted to me all the way down. He's come to stay with his parents for Christmas.'

'Great,' Jayne said as she pulled away. The story would keep Flora busy for the journey home, with any luck.

Jayne sounded the horn as she pulled up outside Sea Haven and Dan came to the door as arranged.

'Well, look at you,' Flora cried out. 'Oh, my dear boy — back on your feet at last! Come here and let me look at you. You're definitely thinner. We need to feed you up a bit.'

'No way. I've been on a strict diet to lose weight so I don't put too much strain on my legs,' said Dan. 'Now, come on in. I need to sit down before I fall down. It's still very early days for walking around.'

'Now, you just tell me whenever you need help. I'm here for you now. Bring my bag in, will you, dear?' she called back to Jayne.

'Don't get cross,' Jayne told herself fiercely. 'Having Flora happy is worth a great deal more than having her annoyed.' Fixing her smile, Jayne carried the heavy suitcase indoors.

'Doesn't everywhere look lovely and festive?' Flora chirped.

'Jayne's worked hard, hasn't she?' said Dan.

'I'm sure it was a team effort. Oh,

lovely, tea and scones. I must give you my new recipe, Jayne dear — the vicar made special reference to them at the church fête this year.'

Dan winked at Jayne, and she managed to keep smiling.

'Thank you, Flora. That would be nice. But I hope these will do for now.'

'And where are my grandchildren? Still banished to the attic?'

'They're only let out twice a year for baths,' Dan told her. 'I think they're down in the village with friends.'

★ ★ ★

Christmas Day finally dawned clear and cold. Presents were piled up under the tree and the children were up early, eager to see what they'd been given, exclaiming with delight as they opened each parcel.

It was a happy hour or two as the family sat chatting together, exchanging gifts.

Chloe had helped Dan to choose a

present for Jayne, who was absolutely thrilled with the antique necklace he'd given her.

'Oh, Dan, it's gorgeous, but you shouldn't have spent so much.'

'I didn't. I sent Chloe in to bargain with the salesman. I think five minutes more and he'd have paid her to take it, just to get rid of her.'

'Your Great-Uncle Henry would never pay the correct price for anything,' Flora put in unexpectedly. 'He was so embarrassing.'

'Here's to Great-Uncle Henry,' Chloe said happily, raising her mug of coffee. 'Now, if you'll excuse me for a while, I'm going to meet Mike. He's joining the frostbite surfers and I'm in charge of the Thermos. See you all at one-thirty for lunch.'

'That girl does not improve,' sighed Flora.

'I think Chloe's great,' Sarah said fiercely. 'I hope she never improves if it means changing her.'

They all laughed, and Jayne went to

organise the turkey, insisting everyone else keep out of her way.

★ ★ ★

Later, as they finished off the last piece of Christmas pudding, Dan rose to his feet, wobbling slightly.

'I'd like to make a speech,' he announced, and then went on, 'This has been such a difficult year for us all. We bought this house with the intention of beginning a new life. I hadn't quite intended the new beginning to be the way it turned out, but with everyone's help and support, here we are.

'We have a beautiful home and a new and thriving business thanks to my wonderful wife, my fantastic children, and their ability to adapt to difficult circumstances.'

The two children looked down at their plates, feeling slightly guilty about their behaviour at times.

'I'd also like to thank my scatty sister

and her amazing bargaining powers — not to mention her deft hand at tiling. Oh, yes, I've heard all about your new-found talent and the excellent tutor you had in Mike.'

Dan raised his glass to Mike and Chloe, and Chloe smiled, looking unexpectedly shy.

'If we're making speeches,' she said, 'then this seems the right moment . . . Mike and I have an announcement to make. We're engaged. He asked me this morning and of course I said yes.'

A glad cry went up and Chloe and Mike were kissed and hugged by everyone in turn.

'Oh, I'm so happy for you both.' Jayne was delighted.

Flora huffed and puffed a little — 'Chloe, settle down? I'll believe it when I see it!' — but she couldn't conceal the real pleasure that she felt.

'So, where will you live?' Dan asked. 'What do you plan to do?'

'Well — if possible — we wondered if you'd consider letting us convert one of your outbuildings into a cottage?' Mike asked tentatively. 'We can't afford to buy it from you, not at first, but if we could rent it from you, maybe some day we could pay for it properly.'

'What a brilliant idea. I'm sure we can come to terms one way or another.' Dan smiled at Mike.

Mike beamed back at him. 'Oh, thank you so much, Mr Pearson! My dad will help with the building work, and once I'm qualified, I'll start looking for jobs around here. I reckon I might set up on my own after a while and see how it goes.'

'What a Christmas this is turning out to be!' said Jayne. 'Tell you what — I've got a bottle of bubbly in the fridge that I bought to celebrate our new home. I'll go and get it — we've got a whole lot more to celebrate now.'

They all raised their glasses.

'Let's drink a toast!' said Jayne. 'To Dan's recovery, to Mike and Chloe's engagement, to Sea Haven, and to everyone connected to it.'

'To us!' everyone agreed.

'And Merry Christmas!' said Flora, smiling.

THE END

We do hope that you have enjoyed reading this large print book.

Did you know that all of our titles are available for purchase?

We publish a wide range of high quality large print books including:
Romances, Mysteries, Classics
General Fiction
Non Fiction and Westerns

Special interest titles available in large print are:
The Little Oxford Dictionary
Music Book, Song Book
Hymn Book, Service Book

Also available from us courtesy of Oxford University Press:
Young Readers' Dictionary
(large print edition)
Young Readers' Thesaurus
(large print edition)

For further information or a free brochure, please contact us at:
Ulverscroft Large Print Books Ltd.,
The Green, Bradgate Road, Anstey,
Leicester, LE7 7FU, England.
Tel: (00 44) **0116 236 4325**
Fax: (00 44) **0116 234 0205**

Other titles in the
Linford Romance Library:

FOREVER IN MY HEART

Joyce Johnson

With the support of a loving family, Julie Haywood is coping well with the trauma of divorce and the difficulties of single parenthood. Well on track with her medical career, she is looking forward to an exciting new promotion — not realising it will bring her into contact with Rob, a part of her past she has tried to forget. Then, when ex-husband Geoff turns up, Julie finds she has some hard decisions to make . . .